BEST OF FRENCH FAIRY TALES FOLK TALES

translated
by S. Novikov

Cherbourg-Octeville : S. Novikov, 2023

The tales in this book do not have one common author—these are French folk stories composed by French people over many centuries. This book presents the best fairy tales of France, which have never appeared in this printed translation before.

What makes them especially valuable as folk work is that they were recorded as narrated by French families, the way they have been told from generation to generation. Grandmothers have been telling some of them to their grandchildren, without the tales ever having been published even in France.

This book does not contain scenes of violence or shocking plots.

The best fairy tales have been selected—amusing, safe, and not in the least scary!

The book includes more than 110 illustrations.

The latest version of the book in a hard copy can be found at the following locations:

www.amazon.com/dp/1792730764
www.amazon.com/dp/170376997X
www.amazon.com/dp/1651023417
www.amazon.com/dp/B07SJ8ZB8Z
www.amazon.co.uk/dp/B07SJ8ZB8Z

This book contains illustrations by artists from all over France. The images thus convey the spirit of each part of the country. The illustrations to Tales 1–23 reflect the vision of artists from Burgundy; 24–30 - from Brittany; 31–35 - from Aquitaine; 36–37 - from Lorraine; 38–40 - from Auvergne; 41–42 - from Alsace; 43–47 - from Franche-Comté. No part of this publication may be distributed, or transmitted in any form or by any means, including photocopying, recording, or other electronic or mechanical methods, without the prior written permission of the publisher, except for brief quotations.
All rights reserved. Copyright © 2020 Sergiy Novikov

ISBN-13: 9798624087545

Other books from this series can be found at
the following locations:

Best of Polish Fairy Tales
www.amazon.com/dp/1517196353

Reading these fairy tales, you will enjoy the wisdom and life experience of many generations of Polish people that are behind them.
The book includes more than 100 illustrations.

In Desert and Wilderness,
The Story of a Lighthouse Keeper
by Henryk Sienkiewicz
www.amazon.com/dp/1530494303

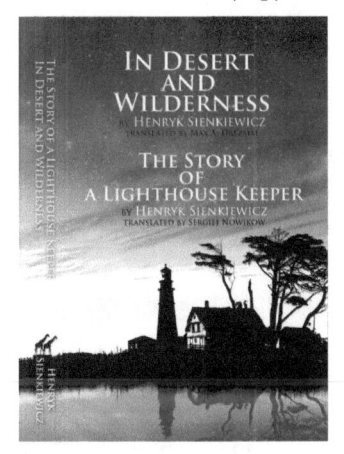

In Desert and Wilderness.
The book describes the wanderings of two children in Africa. It is a fascinating narrative full of adventure.

The Story of a Lighthouse Keeper.
It is an overwhelming story of a retired elderly Soldier who takes the job of a lighthouse keeper in the Caribbean Sea. This is the translation by S. Nowikow, which is easy to read and understand. It is one of the best translations of the work ever published. Henryk Sienkiewicz is the 1905 laureate of the Nobel Prize in Literature.

CONTENTS

1. The Small People 6
2. The Soup Whip 14
3. The Clever Girl 20
4. Léon the Dog and Praline the Cat 24
5. The Straw and the Tar 28
6. The Giant Frog 30
7. Where's the Second Turkey? 32
8. Jean and Jacques Catch the Moon 34
9. The Old Man and the Tree 36
10. Sea of Tulips 40
11. How Many Legs Does the Goose Have? 44
12. Pierre and His Dog 46
13. The Dragon from Tarascon 52
14. The King's Lace 56
15. Ball of Wool 60
16. Why the Rabbit Does Not Talk 64
17. The Large Stove 66
18. The Lost Compote 70
19. Three Artful Sons 72
20. The Careless Wife 76
21. The Cherry Tree 78
22. Two Old Soldiers 80
23. Bernique! Bernaque! 84

24. How the Moon Fell in Love with the Sun 89
25. The Boys of Mayenne 92
26. The Dog and the Moon 94
27. An Incident in the Bois de Boulogne 96
28. The Bird Named It's Mine 98
29. The Little Bird 100
30. The Eagle and the Cock 104

31. The Maid and the Princess 106
32. The Mean Joker 110
33. The Poor Widow, Her Son,
and Cabécou the Goat 112
34. The Pilot from Boulogne 116
35. Life before Birth 120

36. Captain La Ramée's Adventures 122
37. How Sheep Crossed the River 126

38. Vivienne and the Sun 128
39. Jean the Fool 130
40. The Beautiful Princess, the Brave Kitten,
and the Dragon 134

41. The King's Counsellor 138
42. How the Caterpillar Turned into a Butterfly 142

43. The Bear and the Fox 146
44. The Fox and the Tit 148
45. The Hedgehog and the Chestnut Shell 150
46. Biron 154
47. Jean the Thumbling, the Wolf,
and the Robbers 158

The Small People

THE SMALL PEOPLE

I

In mountain caves and under the ground, there lives a tribe of small people called dwarfs.

Dwarfs are up to one foot tall. They have long hair and long beards. They wear fluffy caps, red suits, and boots of silver. They are armed with sabers and spears. The small people are not Christians. They will live until the end of the world. They won't arise from the dead on the Judgement Day.

The dwarfs are not mean; they even do services to humans. But if you want to see their faces get red with anger, just honk like a goose. The dwarfs hate geese because geese always bite dwarfs hard. If you want to see dwarfs as merry as a lark, just say, "You'll get money today."

Humans used to see dwarfs occasionally in the old times. Nothing is heard of them now. Maybe they have left our country. Or maybe they don't dare to come out in the daytime because they are afraid of mean people and goose because they would hurt them.

The dwarfs eat and drink just like we do. I'll tell you how they get what they need.

The land gives us something new every month of the year. It is hay in June, crops in July, grapes and corn in September. It also gives us fruits, each in due season, and cattle, big and small. These are all for us Christians. We can see and touch the gifts of the land whenever we want to.

But there are other crops, other fruits, and other cattle, big and small. Christians can neither see nor touch those, for the land yields them for the small people on a single evening, on New Year's Eve, from sunset to midnight. Everything has to be collected and stacked under the ground before the sun rises.

So the dwarfs have to work really hard for seven hours. They have just an hour more to take out and air their gold in the daylight, for they keep mountains of Louis d'ors and Spanish gold coins in the rocks. If the gold doesn't get some light once a year, it goes bad and red in color. Then the dwarfs don't value it anymore and throw it away.

II

Once upon a time, there was a weaver in Saint-Avit. He had a big family and was as poor as a church mouse. His real name was Cluzet. But when he grew rich, people who envied him nicknamed him Dung Gold. My grandfather—God rest his soul—would often tell me about the weaver who became rich. You will hear the story, too.

Cluzet was a rabbit hunter. Nobody could use a drawnet or a ferret so skillfully, or shoot from an ambush even in the darkest nights, in any time of the year.

He killed more than a thousand little animals in his life. His wife and daughter would sell them at the market or at fairs in Lectoure and Astaffort.

Noble gentlemen and rich citizens who liked rabbit hunting were angry with Cluzet. They called him cheat and poacher and tried to set gendarmes at him. Cluzet only laughed at it because he often supplied judges in Lectoure with delicious rabbit stew for a good price. Of course, the gentlemen did not feel like judging a useful man like Cluzet.

On a winter evening, shortly before New Year, Cluzet had soup in his family circle, as was his habit. Having finished the supper, he said to his wife, "Listen, Wifey! Tomorrow is the day when you give New Year presents. I want to present several rabbits to the bosses in Lectoure. Put the children to bed and go to sleep yourself. I'll go hunting."

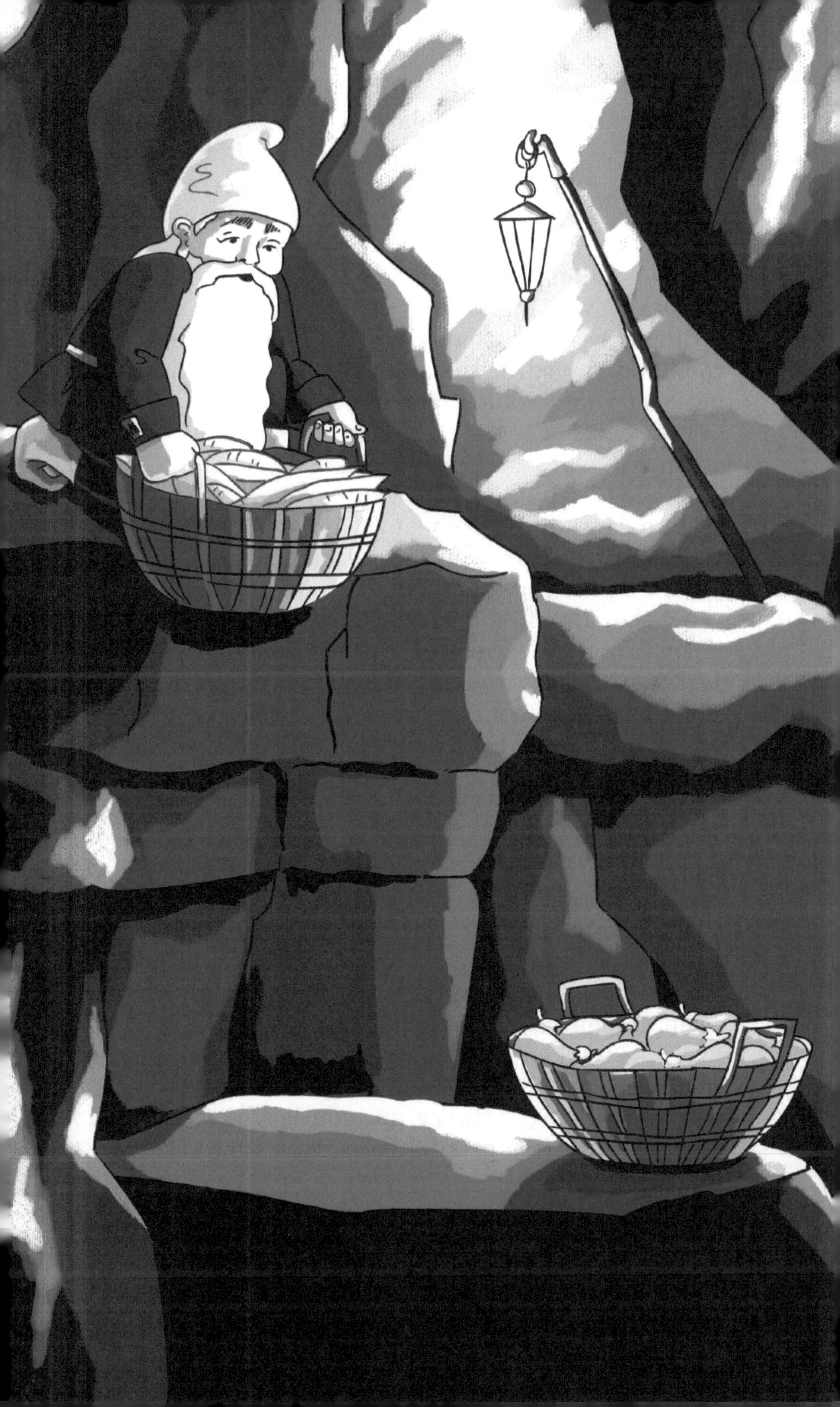

Cluzet took his gun and a bag and left. It was chilly outside, and stars were shining in the moonless black sky.

Hardly had our weaver hidden between the rocks when he heard somebody shout under his feet, "Hurry up, you lazybones! Everything must be ready at midnight sharp!" "We know, Ruler! This New Year's Eve is the only night that we have!"

Cluzet realized that the dwarfs were preparing to work and stayed in the ambush. He was curious to see and hear what would come next.

The chief of the dwarfs appeared at the cave entrance, whip in hand, glanced at the sky, and shouted, "Midnight! Hurry up, you lazy things! You have to carry our yearly stock underground before the sun rises." "Your word is our command, Ruler! We only have one night in a year."

As the dwarf ruler was cracking his whip, herds of small people swarmed out of the cave. They were carrying scythes, reaping hooks, flails, garden knives, grape baskets, shoulder yokes, and picking sticks—all the things needed to harvest crops and drive cattle together.

After the people disappeared, their ruler shouted to the weaver, "Cluzet, would you like a six-livre coin?" "Sure, Mr. Dwarf!" "Then help my people, Cluzet." Some of the dwarfs were back after an hour.

Some were carrying carts the size of half a pumpkin, loaded with hay, grapes, corn, and fruit. Others were driving bulls and cows the size of a dog and flocks of sheep as small as a weasel.

Cluzet worked hard to help the dwarfs. Hundreds of them were arriving. The dwarf ruler was cracking his whip and saying, "Hurry up, you lazybones! The stock must be under the ground before the sunrise!" "We *are* hurrying, Master. We know we only have this night on New Year's Eve."

The dwarfs' stock was all under the ground by the time the sun rose.

The dwarf ruler said to the weaver, "Keep your six livres, Cluzet. You have earned them honestly. Would you like to earn an ecu more?" "Of course I do, Mr. Dwarf!" "So help my people!"

Small people were already emerging from the deep cave, bending under heavy bags with yellow gold, Louis d'ors, and Spanish gold coins. Their ruler kept cracking his whip and saying, "Hurry up, you lazybones! You have just an hour to air the yellow gold. If you don't bring it out to the daylight once a year, it goes bad and gets red in color, and we have to throw it away." "We *are* working, Master. We're doing our best."

Cluzet worked a lot. He poured gold out of the bag and stirred it to make sure all of it got aired and saw some daylight.

As soon as an hour passed, the dwarfs hurried to take their bags of gold back to the cave. Their ruler said with a crack of his whip, "Here's another ecu for you, Cluzet. You have earned it honestly! But my people are bad workers. As much as 350 pounds of yellow gold has not seen the daylight for over a year because of them. It's all got bad and red. You lazy things! Throw it away. I don't want it here."

The dwarfs obeyed. They threw 350 pounds of red gold out of the cave. Then they vanished in the cave along with their ruler.

Cluzet took a Louis d'or and a Spanish gold coin, buried the rest of the gold, and went home.

III

His wife asked him as he arrived, "Was it a good hunt, Hubby?" "It was, Wifey." "Show me what you've got." "Not now. I have to leave on business."

Without even having a meal, Cluzet went to the city of Agen and entered the Goldsmith's shop. "Hello, Goldsmith. Just look at this red gold! Here's a Louis d'or and a Spanish gold coin. They are as valuable as yellow gold, aren't they?" "They are, my friend. If you wish, I can give you an ecu for them."

Having counted the money, Cluzet hurried to Saint-Avit without eating or drinking. By the time he reached his home, he could hardly utter, "Hurry up, Wife, give me some soup. Bread and wine, too. I'm parched with thirst."

Having finished his supper, the weaver went to bed and slept for fifteen hours in a row. But on the following night, without telling anyone, he headed for the rocks to bring a hundred pounds of red gold. He went there two more times that night and took the rest. Having brought all the gold, Cluzet called for wife. "Look! Wasn't I right to say I had a good hunt on New Year's Eve? We're rich now. Let's leave the place and live high!"

So they did. Cluzet and his family left Saint-Avit and went far away, farther than Moissa, to Quercy. Cluzet used his 350 pounds of red gold to buy a big forest, a water mill with four millstones, twenty farms, and a splendid castle, where he lived happily ever after with his wife and children. He was a nice man, eager to help his neighbors and very generous to the poor. People envied him anyway, so they called him Dung Gold.

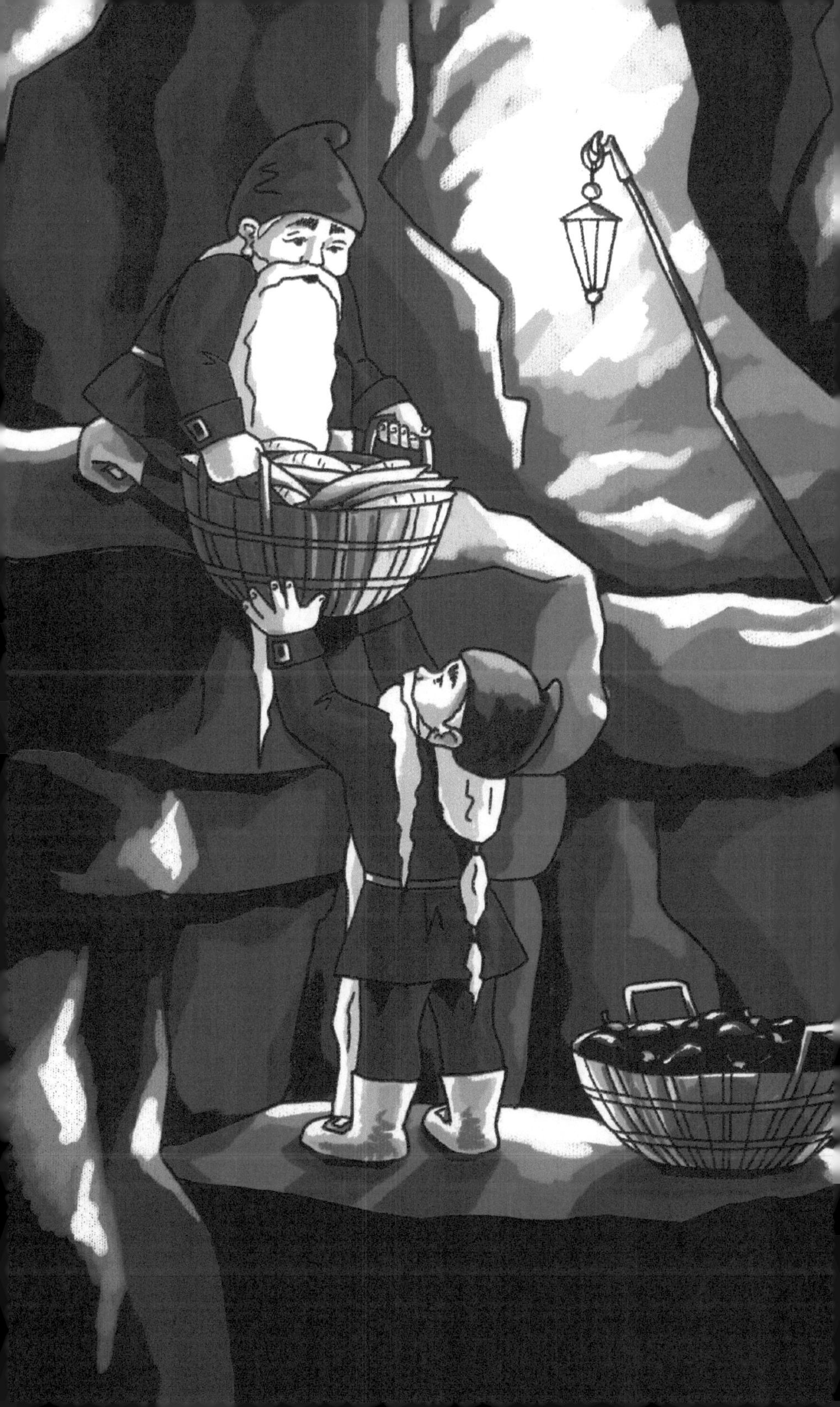

The Soup Whip

THE SOUP WHIP

I

In the Kingdom of Grape Stones, there lived the silliest king in the world.

The King had a Gardener, who was very merry and cunning.

Unfortunately, the King married a clever beautiful girl from a nearby kingdom. But his servants were silly, and so were his horses and dogs. The young beauty was very bored.

Once she fell very ill. She would not eat, or drink, or laugh. She was going to die of boredom.

The silly King was scared. What could he do to heal his wife? He called the best doctors, but they were silly, so nobody could not think of a cure. A doctor from another kingdom chanced to be staying there. Having examined the Queen, he said, "She is dying of boredom, Your Majesty. We have to make her laugh. Nothing else will help."

So the silly King and his silly councilors tried to make the Queen laugh. But all their ideas were silly. Silly things are only funny when clever people invent them. When a fool does silly things, it's boring. The King and his councilors tried every thing, but the beautiful Queen would not even smile.

II

Disappointed, the King decided to have a walk in the garden. He came across the Gardener. The Gardener was in a good mood. He was watering the roses and humming a song. His giggly wife was looking at him out of the window of their tiny house and screaming with laughter.

This made the silly King angry. "How dare you laugh when sadness and boredom reign in my kingdom!

Don't you sing! And forbid your wife to laugh! I'll tonight to make sure you obey my order!"

"Alright," the Gardener thought with a hidden smile, "We'll see."

But he said with a respectful bow, "Your order is my command!"

III

The Gardener was going to have supper with his wife. She had just put a pot with soup in it on the fire. Hardly had the soup begun to boil when the Gardener saw the King approaching.

"Hide and keep silent!" he shouted to his wife. He hurried to put out the fire, placed the pot in the middle of the room, grabbed a whip and began to lash the pot hard.

On entering the house, the King froze. He saw the Gardener lashing a pot in the center of the room, repeating, "One has to be clever to cook soup without any fire."

The King asked him, 'What are you doing?"

The Gardener replied with a bow, "Sorry, Your Majesty. I wanted to make a treat for you but my wife's out. So I have to cook soup on my own."

"How can you cook it without fire?"

"Simple as that. I inherited the pot from my Grandmother and the whip from my Grandfather. If you put vegetables, roots, and water into the pot, it will cook soup without any fire. Only you have to lash it hard with this whip, or it will get lazy."

The King rushed to take off the lid. Indeed, the soup was steaming hot and delicious! It occurred to him that the Queen might find it entertaining.

The King begged, "Please give me this pot and this whip!"

The Gardener wouldn't agree. At last, he said, "Alright, Your Majesty. Take my whip and pot. Only give me the fastest horse for the whip and a bag of silver for the pot."

The King ordered for the best horse and a bag of silver for the Gardener. He took the whip and the pot— he poured out the soup—and hurried to the palace.

IV

The silly King gathered his court people and servants. They went to the Queen. He put the pot in the middle of the room and said, "I'm going to show you how the soup whip works. Nobody has seen anything of the kind! I'm going to cook it without any fire!"

The beautiful Queen smiled because she knew that one cannot cook soup without fire.

In the meanwhile, the King poured some water into the pot, added meat, vegetables, and salt, then put the lid on. "Look!" he said and started whipping the pot.

He whipped and whipped and whipped and whipped it. He got tired, but the pot remained cold.

The Queen looked at him with a smile.

The silly King continued to lash the pot. He whipped and whipped and whipped and whipped and whipped it. He was sweating heavily, but the pot was no warmer than it had been.

Looking at the King, the Queen said laughingly, "Where did you get the pot and the whip, Your Majesty?"

"From the Gardener. I exchanged my fastest horse for the whip and a bag of silver for the pot."

This made the Queen roar with laughter. How cunning the Gardener was! Then she said,

"Maybe it is because of some special words that the Gardener said that the pot cooked soup, Your Majesty?"

"Indeed," said the King, "he said, one has to be clever to cook soup without any fire."

The Queen could not resist it anymore. She had not laughed so desperately since she was a child. Then she said, "The Gardener fooled you! Give me a horse. I will chase him!"

V

"Hurry up!" the silly King shouted, "A horse for the Queen!"

The Queen ran out of the palace, mounted the horse, and galloped along the road that the Gardener and his giggly wife had taken.

Only the beauty was not chasing them. She was just sick of living among silly people, so she returned to her father.

The silly King stood in front of the cold pot for a while. Then he thought, "If they say that one has to be clever to cook soup without any fire, I have to cook it, or they will think that I'm a fool."

So he began to whip the pot. He whipped and whipped and whipped and whipped and whipped and whipped it... When he was too tired to continue, he gave the whip to his son, who passed it over to his own son. All kings of the Kingdom of Grape Stones have been lashing the soup whip since then. The pot won't get any warmer, though.

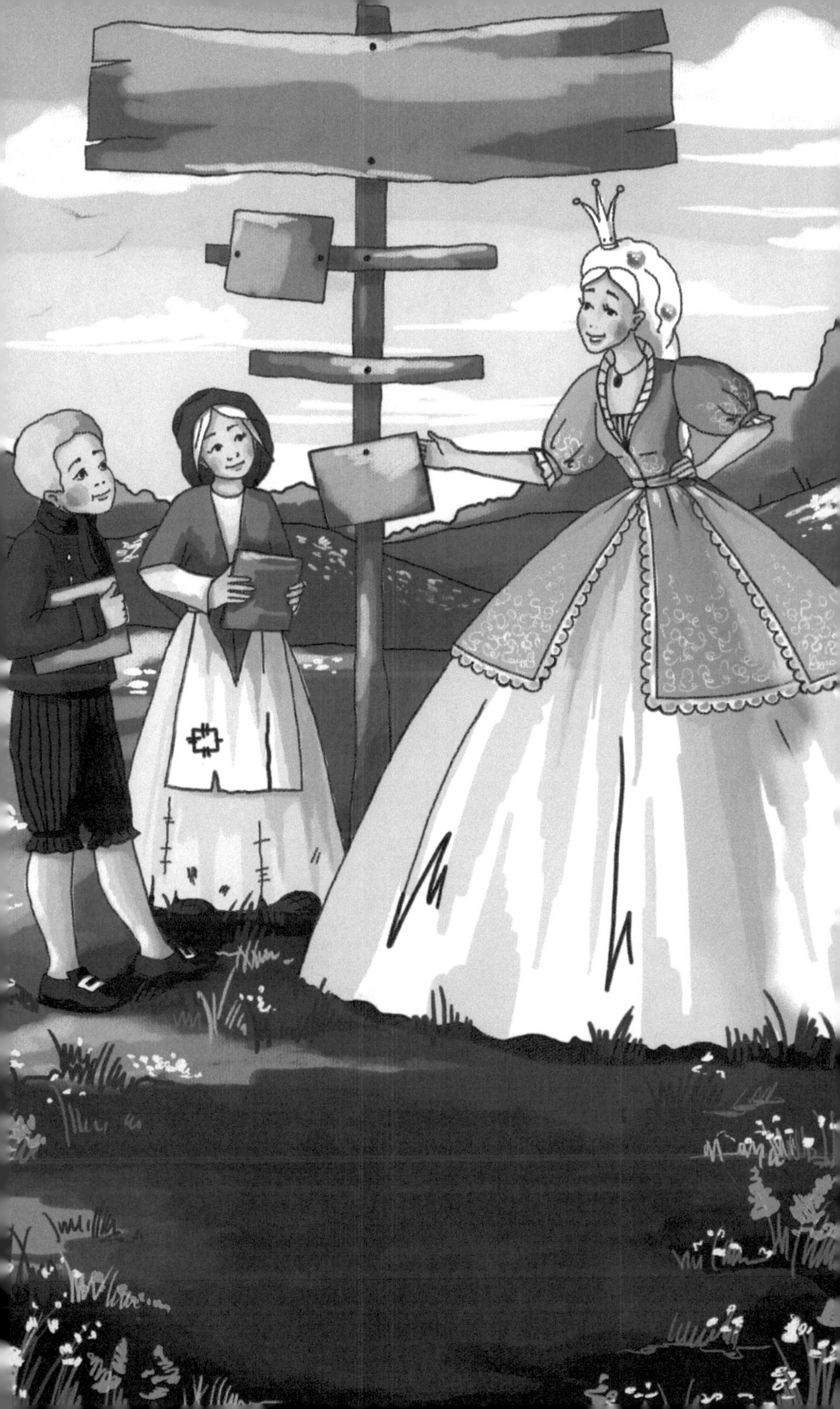

The Clever Girl

THE CLEVER GIRL

Once upon a time there lived an old King. He had always been a fair and circumspect ruler. The country had been going stronger year by year. Now that the treasury was full of gold, the King decided to reward the most intelligent of his subjects. But how could he find out who was the most intelligent?

He called his scribe and dictated to him the most sophisticated riddles that he knew. The news travelled across the country soon, and a crowd gathered in front of his palace. All those people believed themselves to be really clever. Yet, two days passed without a single riddle being solved.

A girl turned up on the third day. She was wearing rugged clothes. She looked very young, but her eyes were wonderfully intelligent. Finally, she was invited to see the King. The King was surprised to see such a young girl. "She must be very brave," he thought.

"Don't you think, child, that you can't compete with the crowd of learned and sharp-witted people whom I have sent back home empty-handed?"

"Why, Your Majesty. While the eyes are afraid, the feet walk where one orders them. So I am here," the girl replied to the King.

"Alright. Here's my first question. What is it that smooths out any distance and obeys no orders?"

"Your Majesty, *love smooths out any distance*[1]. *Love obeys no orders.*[2]"

---
[1] Translator's note: This is a translation of the French expression: "L'amour rapproche les distances."
The French original of all proverbs and set expressions used here appears in footnotes.
[2] L'amour ne se commande pas.

"Well done! You're so wise as for a young girl," the King was surprised. "Tell me, dear, who are the world's best doctors?"

"There are three, Your Majesty. *The best doctors are Dr. Good Mood, Dr. Diet, and Dr. Rest.*[3]"

"I've been disputing it with my court people whether one should repay evil with good. What do you think?"

"They say in my village, *do good to a dog and it'll piss on you*[4]. But I don't think so. *One should repay evil with good.*[5]"

"You're right again. Here's my last question: What can't one conceal for a long time?"

"Well, *one cannot conceal love, fire, and cough for a long time*[6]."

The King was astonished to see the girl answer the questions that many learned men had failed to answer. He wanted to put one last tricky question to her.

"What can make my subjects kinder and wealthier? They often quarrel with each other. They also keep coming to me for money, which I don't like."

"The answer is as simple as that, Your Majesty. *Work wades off three great evils—enemies, vices, and poverty.*[7] Your court people should not reject any work. *All occupations are good. There is no bad trade; there are only stupid people.*[8]"

"You're so much more than a simple girl! A treasure of a girl you are! All my gold is not worth your wisdom. But I'm going to keep my promise and give you a generous reward."

The girl said thank you, took her reward, and returned home. Her poor parents were waiting for her. At last they had enough money to build a warm house.

---

[3] Les meilleurs médecins sont le Dr. Gai, le Dr. Diète et le Dr. Tranquille.
[4] Faites du bien à un chien, il vous pisse contre.
[5] Faut rendre le bien pour le mal.
[6] Amour, toux, fumée, et argent ne ce peuvent cacher longtemps.
[7] Le travail éloigne de nous trois grand maux - l'ennemi, la vice et le besoin.
[8] Tous les métiers sont bons. Il n'y a pas de sots métiers, il y a de sottes gens.

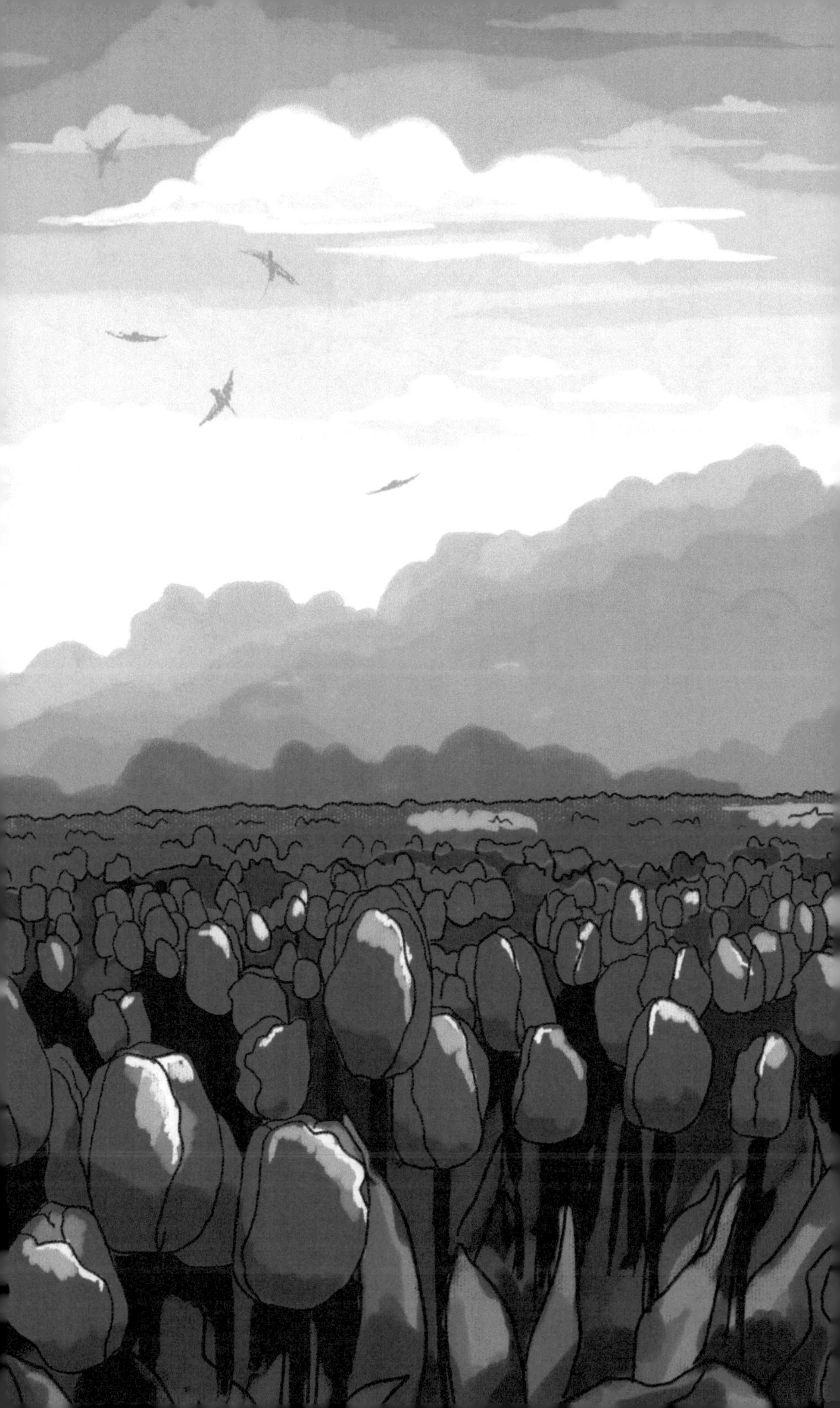

Léon the Dog and Praline the Cat

LÉON THE DOG AND PRALINE THE CAT

An old woman had a dog and a cat. The Dog's name was Léon and the Cat's Praline.

Léon and Praline got on well. The Dog would bark at passers-by and the Cat catch mice. The two of them cuddled at their owner's feet while she slept in her rocking chair.

Once, the Cat did not feel like catching mice. He waited till the old lady fell asleep and sneaked into the cellar to get some cream.

"Wonderful," the Cat though as he licked his long whiskers clean of the fat cream, "A delicious meal at no cost."

Praline began to steal cream every day. He got extremely fat and lazy.

"The Cat's life is a bed of roses," it occurred to Léon. "I don't want to work anymore."

So the Dog slept in his kennel for days without showing anywhere.

The old lady could not stand it anymore. She called her lazy servants and said, "I'll give roasted chicken to the one who works well tonight."

She showed them the chicken before hiding it in the cupboard. Their mouths watered. The two of them decided to compete.

Léon spent the night barking. Praline tried to catch a mouse but failed because he had forgotten how to do it.

"Léon is a good barker," the cat thought. "He's going to get the chicken."

He was so disappointed that he could not keep from sneaking into the cupboard. He gulped down the chicken.

In the morning, the old lady found the Cat asleep and decided to give the treat to the Dog. When she saw the chicken gone, she understood at once who was to blame. She grabbed a stick, but the Cat ran away.

The Dog got angry because he had been barking hard to no avail. He jumped at the Cat and bit his tail.

This is why cats and dogs always fight.

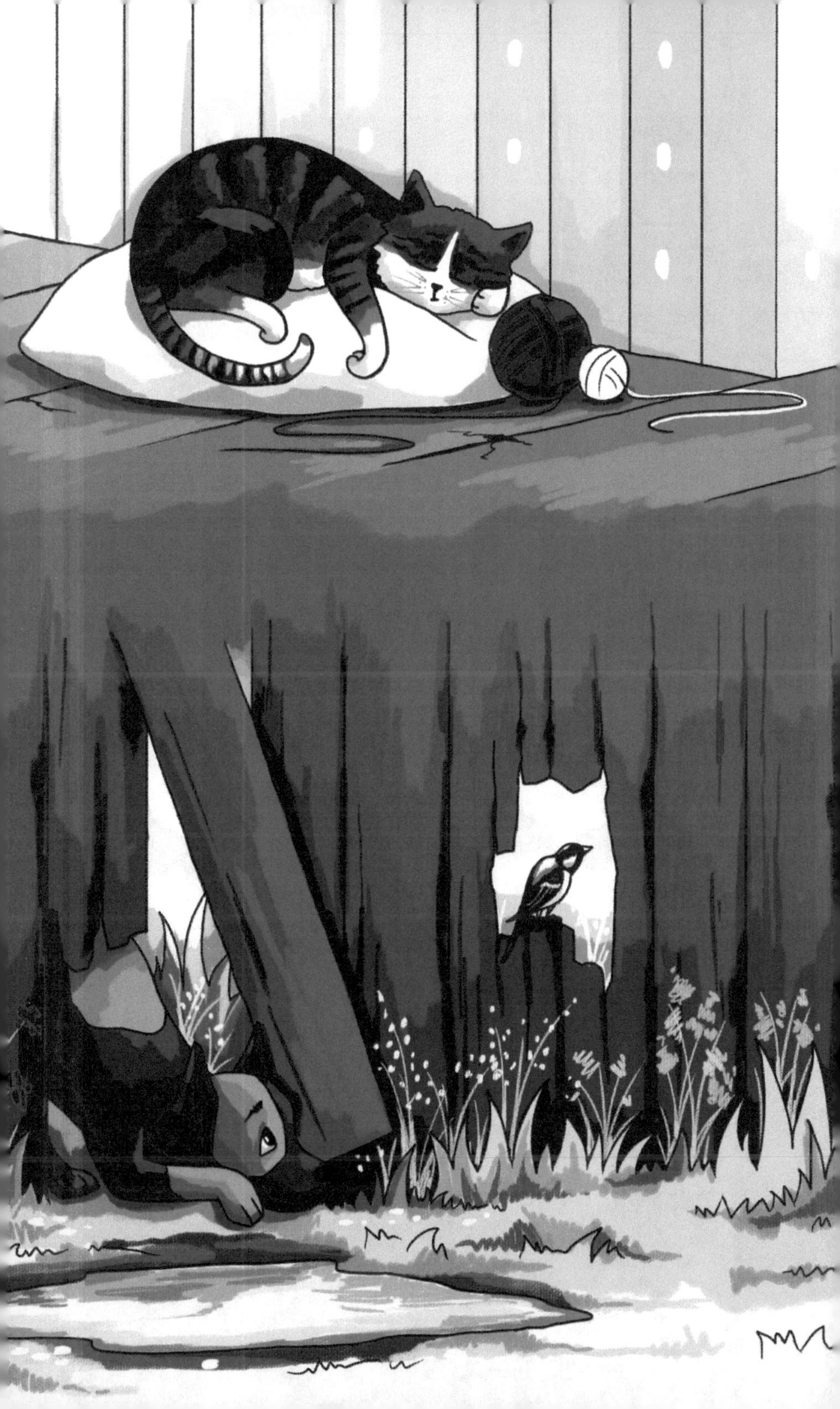

The Straw and the Tar

THE STRAW AND THE TAR

Once the Straw and the Tar had an argument. The Straw said that it burned better and produced more heat. The Tar believed itself to burn slowly but much hotter. They could not settle it themselves and had to ask passers-by.

A Father and his Son happened to be walking by. It was chilly, and they were very cold. The Son said, "Let's burn some straw to get warmer, shall we?"

"I'd rather burn tar," the Father replied.

The Son set fire to the Straw, anyway. Thinking that it was the best burner, it flared happily for a moment and went out. The Father set fire to the Tar. It proved to be a slow burner and produced enough heat for the Father and the Son to get nice and warm.

The Giant Frog

THE GIANT FROG

Once a long time ago, a heavy drought came.

Every river dried out. Even clouds were gone. The soil was as hard as a rock. The cracks in it were often too wide to jump over. Granaries were growing empty. People and animals were looking at the hot scorching sun in terror.

It turned out that the Frog had drunk all the water. She was monstrously big. People and animals gathered together to think of a way to fill back rivers and lakes.

It occurred to them that making the Frog laugh could be a good idea. But funny jokers, leaping hares, and dancing cranes all failed. The Frog would not open her mouth.

A little boy came up with a solution. He got a little worm and put it onto the giant Frog's belly. As the worm slithered around, its tail tickled the Frog.

Finally, she could not stand it anymore and burst into laughter. Everything echoed with her roar. Her mouth was pouring a waterfall.

Soon, clouds appeared in the sky. It started to rain at last. The ground became softer, and people took to sowing their fields happily.

This is how a smart little boy saved the whole country.

Where's the Second Turkey?

WHERE'S THE SECOND TURKEY?

It was the custom in a city to give two turkeys to the man who did one a favor. One was for 'Thank you', and the second a reward.

Once a man sent two turkeys to his neighbor by messenger. The messenger could not resist to call at an inn and drink one of the turkeys away. So he only delivered one.

"Where's the second turkey?" asked the receiver.

"This is the second one," the messenger replied.

"I ask you, where's the second turkey?"

"I tell you, this is the second one."

The receiver got angry. He knocked at his neighbor's door and said, "You've told me thank you alright, but why did you only give me one turkey? Was my help of no use to you?"

"Why? I sent two, I swear!"

The two of them looked at the messenger and demanded, "You **must** tell where the second turkey is."

He kept saying that was the second one. They got furious and sent him away.

The messenger drudged away, grumbling, "Why do they keep asking about the second turkey... I'd have told them the truth if they had asked where the **first** turkey was."

Jean and Jacques Catch the Moon

JEAN AND JACQUES CATCH THE MOON

Once upon a time, it occurred to Jean and Jacque that they could catch the golden moon and bring it to the King. The King would probably give them money and land.

Having found a big pot with a lid and a long stick, they set off.

It was night when they finally climbed the top of a high hill. Jean said to Jacques, "Look! How low the moon hangs! Let's use the stick!"

They lifted the stick to the sky but could not reach the moon. They merely hit a couple of stars.

They looked around and saw a tall tree. Jacques said to Jean, "Look! What a tall tree! Go climb it. I'll be down there, holding the pot open for the moon."

Jean climbed the tree. When he was on the top, he shouted, "I can't reach it!" "Jump, will you?" his friend suggested, opening the pot.

The moon hid behind a cloud. Jean made a jump and tumbled into the pot. Seeing that it was dark and the pot was full, Jacques put on the lid and shouted, "I've got it!"

Jacques brought the pot to the palace. When he opened it in front of the King, Jean appeared.

"Do you think I don't know the difference between a man and the moon?" the King shouted angrily.

Things looked blue, but Jean said to the King, "This is why the moon disappears in the daytime, Your Majesty. It turns into a man."

This made the King laugh. He set the two friends free but warned them that **they would have to work hard and not catch the moon if they wanted to become rich.**

The Old Man and the Tree

THE OLD MAN AND THE TREE

Once the King was traveling with his glittering retinue and saw a very old man planting an olive tree.

"Hey there, Gray Beard," the King said. "Do you think you'll live to see the tree fruit?"

"Oh Greatest Ruler," he replied. "This is the ancient custom. Some are to plant the tree and others to take the fruits. Yet, old as I am, I might hopefully live to see this tree fruit."

The King appreciated the wise reply, so he threw a purse full of money to the old man.

"See," the old man smiled, "it's already fruiting."

The King burst out laughing and threw him another purse.

"Oh, Your Majesty! Trees normally fruit once a year. Mine does it twice!"

The King liked this joke even more and threw another purse to the old man.

"Thank you, Master! I'll use the money to plant more olive trees so that the fruits are enough for many people and not only my children and grandchildren."

"Why work this hard? You've got a lot of money now. You'll always have a crust till your dying day."

"By working we express our love for our neighbors. To earn a living is not the only reason why I work. Being rich does not mean not having to work. My father used to tell me,

37

"*Work wades off three great evils—enemies, vices, and poverty.*[1]" People from my village often said, *"One who does not work does not eat.*[2]"

Here is my answer to your question, Master: *A day without work is a wasted one.*[3]"

---

[1] Le travail éloigne de nous trois grand maux - l'ennemi, la vice et le besoin.
[2] Qui ne travaille pas ne mange pas.
[3] C'est un jour perdu qu'un jour sans travail.

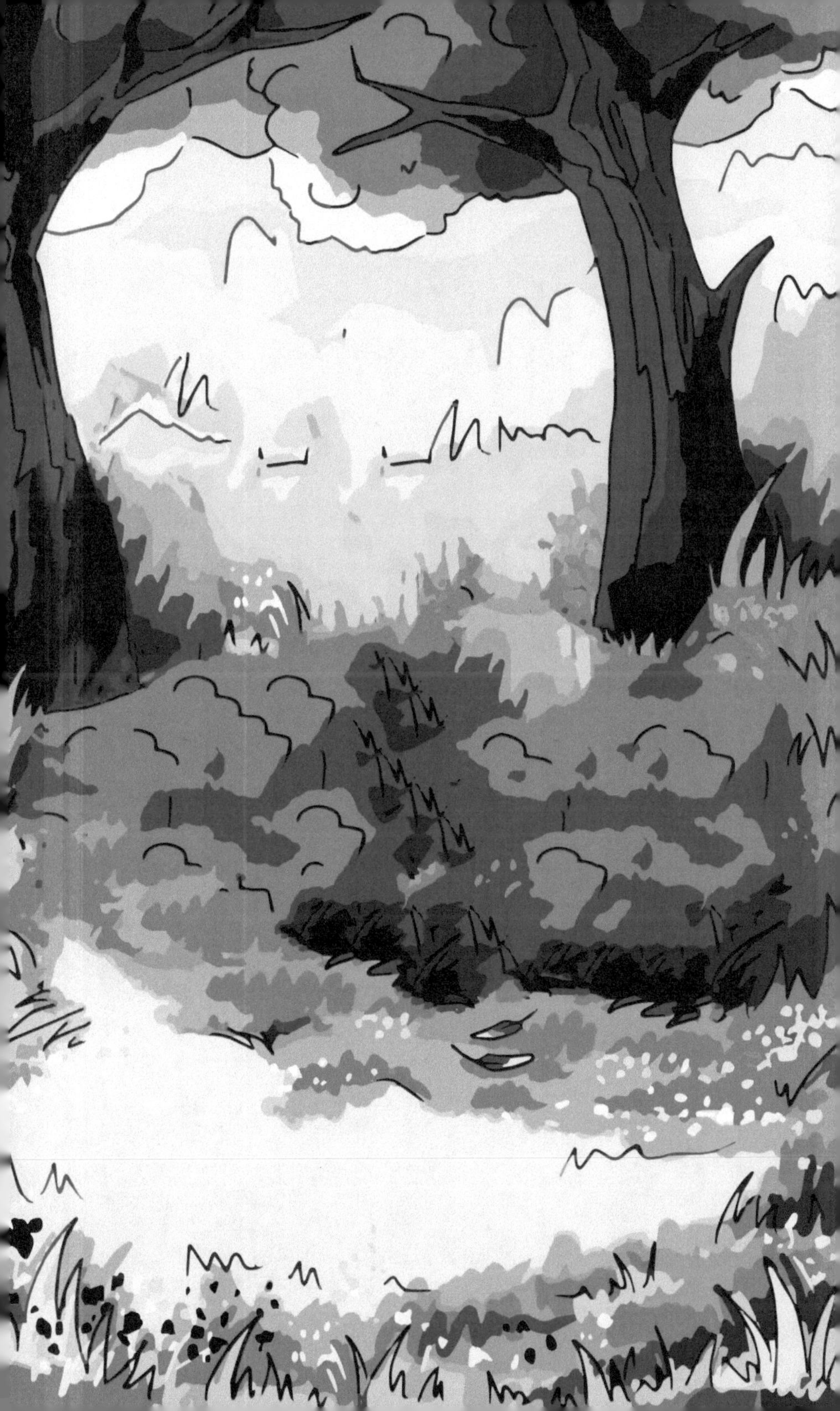

Sea of Tulips

SEA OF TULIPS

A poor shepherd named Eustache lived in a French village.

The shepherd was very young. His heart was not embittered with malice yet; pride and hatred had not withered it. On the contrary, Eustache's heart was very big and untainted. His soul was like an everblooming flower. He had heard about the beautiful feeling of love. Of course he knew what it felt like to love his sheep, his village, his father and mother. Yet, he felt that there was something about love that he didn't know.

Once on a beautiful day, as soon as the first crimson rays of sunset touched the sky, Eustache produced a flute out of his pocket. He played an ancient shepherds' song to drive his flock home. The wind carried the sweet tune across the meadow, lifting it nearly as high as the clouds.

It was not only the nature and the sheep who heard the shepherd play. A beautiful girl was standing on a high hill with her eyes closed, enjoying every sound of it. He hair was fluttering in the wind. The cool breath of the approaching night and the melody coming straight from the boy's heart intertwined with it. She was so beautiful that she looked like a second sun. At seeing her, Eustache felt something unknown arise in his heart. He froze, and the music broke off. The girl opened her eyes and gave him a sweet look.

"This must be the love that I've been looking for. As beautiful and radiant as this strange girl," thought Eustache.

But the girl was gone before he knew it. The boy searched for her across the meadow, but she seemed to have vanished into thin air.

"She'll probably come back tomorrow or the day after tomorrow. She'll be eager to hear my song," the shepherd dreamt on his way home.

He didn't get a wink of sleep that night. Impatience or the new feeling made his heart thump. However, the mysterious stranger did not come back for as long as a week.

Eustache began to ask villagers about her; but nobody was able to help him because the girl had not turned up in the village. The shepherd thought of a special way to show her how much he loved her.

"I'll plough the whole meadow and sow it all with crimson tulips as bright as my love," he decided.

It took the youth three days and three nights to plough the meadow. Eustache was poor and could not afford even a dozen of seeds. Yet, the new feeling of love told him that he was doing the right thing.

On the following morning, Eustache sold his flock to a merchant from abroad and bough 10 bags of perfect tulip bulbs.

He sowed the meadow and began to wait. He would spend every minute on the meadow, praying for rain and soft sunshine. Many days and weeks passed before the thin stalks showed flower buds.

Eustache knew that the meadow would become a vast crimson sea in one day and one night. The fiery petals would be its waves. This is exactly what happened. Yet, the truly miraculous thing about it was the wonderful smell of crimson tulips, which reached even farther than the tune had on the evening when the youth met the beautiful stranger. He believed that she would smell the flowers, see their radiance, and come back to the loving shepherd.

It was not only the girl who saw the vast field of crimson tulips but people came from across the world to admire the wonderful flowers.

Nobody has seen the shepherd in the village since the day the tulips first blossomed. Only his crimson sea of millions of tulips has bloomed every year. They say that the girl was a princess, that the two of them got married—what a beautiful wedding it was!—and live in a palace. People believe that a man capable of sowing a whole field with wonderful flowers must have a wonderful soul and, of course, live a wonderful life.

Flower fields across France still remind us of what Eustache did for his beloved one.

They still say in East France, *"If a flower bloomed each time I think of you, the world would turn into a vast garden.*[1]*"*

---

[1] Si à chaque fois que je pensais à toi une fleur poussait alors le monde serait un grand jardin.

How Many Legs Does the Goose Have?

HOW MANY LEGS DOES THE GOOSE HAVE?

A rich man had a large house and a garden. The man was greedy, so he only had one Servant. This did not prevent him from indulging in every pleasure he could think of. The poor Servant worked his fingers to the bone. He did all the gardening, cooking, and cleaning.

Once the Master ordered his servant to make a pond in the garden. He wanted to have enough geese to eat one for supper every day.

The Servant obeyed. When the geese had grown big enough, he picked the fattest one for roasting. As soon as he produced it out of the oven, the air was thick with a mouthwatering smell. Hungry and tired, the Servant thought, "I've been working hard for my master! I haven't spared myself for years! Don't I deserve a goose leg?"

Having said this, he helped himself to a golden leg.

When supper time came, he served the goose on a tray. Seeing one of the legs gone, the Master grew angry.

"Why, the goose only had one leg," the Servant replied.

"I've never seen a one-legged goose in my whole life!"

"Come to the pond and I'll show you."

The two of them went to the pond. It was a hot day, so all the geese were standing on one leg.

"You see, Master? All the geese are one-legged!"

Suddenly the master shooed the birds. They began to run about.

"You liar! Now they have two legs, don't they?"

"Why didn't you shoo that goose too, Master?" replied the Servant.

Pierre and His Dog

PIERRE AND HIS DOG

ittle Pierre lived at Old Jacques' for 9 years.

Chapter 1. Alone

When his parents died, their neighbors adopted his elder brothers and sisters. Pierre's father, a blacksmith, was a well-respected man. Everybody liked his modest and friendly wife.

However, not a single family in the village could afford another eater in early winter because they could hardly feed their children. Yet, the neighbors knew the blacksmith's sons to be honest and hard-working and his daughters diligent and thrifty.

The neighbors said with a sigh, "Well, they can do housework or get a trade. We can't let them starve." Having said so, they took Pierre's siblings by the hand and brought them to their homes. Some families even adopted two children.

All of Pierre's ten brothers and sisters found a new home. But the three-year-old boy was unwanted. The neighbors heaved another sign, "He can't work and is hard to take care of. We'll help the elder kids. May God help the little one."

They left Pierre all alone in the empty house. He curled up in the warmest corner, near the cooling stove, and fall asleep.

Chapter 2. Rescued

Pierre woke up because somebody was shaking him by the shoulder. He opened his eyes to see Old Jacques, a shepherd who lived on his own in the hills. He spent the summer tending sheep and the winter repairing household stuff for villagers.

Everybody knew him to be a good craftsman and a careful shepherd. He knew a thing or two about pasturing and had not lost a single sheep. But Old Jacques was very unsociable. His gray horse and a shagged mongrel dog were his only friends. He would not invite neighbors to his house or visit theirs. Rumor had it that he had not lost a single sheep in years because he could speak the language that wolves speak and agree with them. Shortly speaking, villagers respected Old Jacques but were suspicious to him.

But Little Pierre was not afraid because Old Jacques produced a large sandwich with ewe's milk cheese from his leather bag and gave it to the boy without saying a word. One isn't expected to be afraid when munching on a delicious sandwich, right?

In the meanwhile, Old Jacques looked around the empty house, took off his sheepskin coat, wrapped Little Pierre in it—all this without producing a sound—and brought him out to the snow-covered street.

Chapter 3. At Home

Pierre had no memory of their sledge trip from the hill to Old Jacque's house. He simply fell asleep. He slept through the blizzard and the shine of the giant moon. He even missed the howl of wolves behind the hill. When they reached Old Jacque's hut, Jean Pierre slept for another day. The shagged mongrel dog lay near. Its breath made Pierre feel warm and comfortable. That was the beginning of their friendship.

In fact, the name of Old Jacque's dog was Friend. The shepherd would grumble occasionally that it was a wrong name because the dog had forgotten his owner completely for the boy.

Old Jacque loved Pierre. He loved his dog named Friend, his gray horse named Helper, and the sheep that he tended during the summer season. He also loved people. He was just incapable of small talk, which villagers enjoyed greatly. He would rather have a silent walk in the hills in the company of Friend and, recently, Pierre, sometimes on Helper, than spend the evening chatting at the inn.

Chapter 4. Life with Old Jacques

As the years went passing by, Pierre came to call Old Jacque Grandpa, and Old Jacque called him Grandson. Grandpa taught Pierre how to find the best pastures, make hay for Helper, do gardening and even some basic shoemaking. On winter evenings, Pierre learned to read, write, and count. Grandpa also taught him geography.

If a villager brought a thing that wanted repair to Old Jacque, Pierre received the guest and did the talking, while Grandpa worked. Customers were more satisfied than before and paid more.

After nine years of such happy living another shift happened in Pierre's life. Grandpa was down with an illness.

"Pierre," Grandpa said, "I'm nearing my end. You'll soon have to return to the village because you're too young to live in the hills on your own. Find a decent family that would adopt you not just because you are a good worker but because they love you." "How do I know?" Pierre asked.

And Grandpa whispered his secret to Pierre.

Chapter 5. Grandpa's Secret

After a week, a tall boy carrying a bag went down to the valley. A gray horse and an old shagged mongrel dog were accompanying him.

It was summer. Every family needed a laborer and invited Pierre to live and work in their house.

"Come," they would say. "You'll sleep not in the hayloft, where laborers sleep, but on clean bedsheets in the house. Just get rid of your dog. Why do you need this useless old thing?"

Pierre never agreed.

"We need a laborer, and we'll pay you as much as we pay to grown-ups," others promised. "Only your dog and horse are good for nothing. Get rid of them, will you?"

Pierre refused.

"Boy," he heard from a modest house on the fringe of the village. "We need a laborer. We can't pay you a lot, but you'll live here as a family member. We've got enough room and food for your dog and horse, too."

"Thank you!" Pierre said with a smile. "I agree. Grandpa told me to find a family that would love me. He said, *one who loves me loves my dog as well.*[1]"

---

[1] Qui m'aime, aime mon chien.

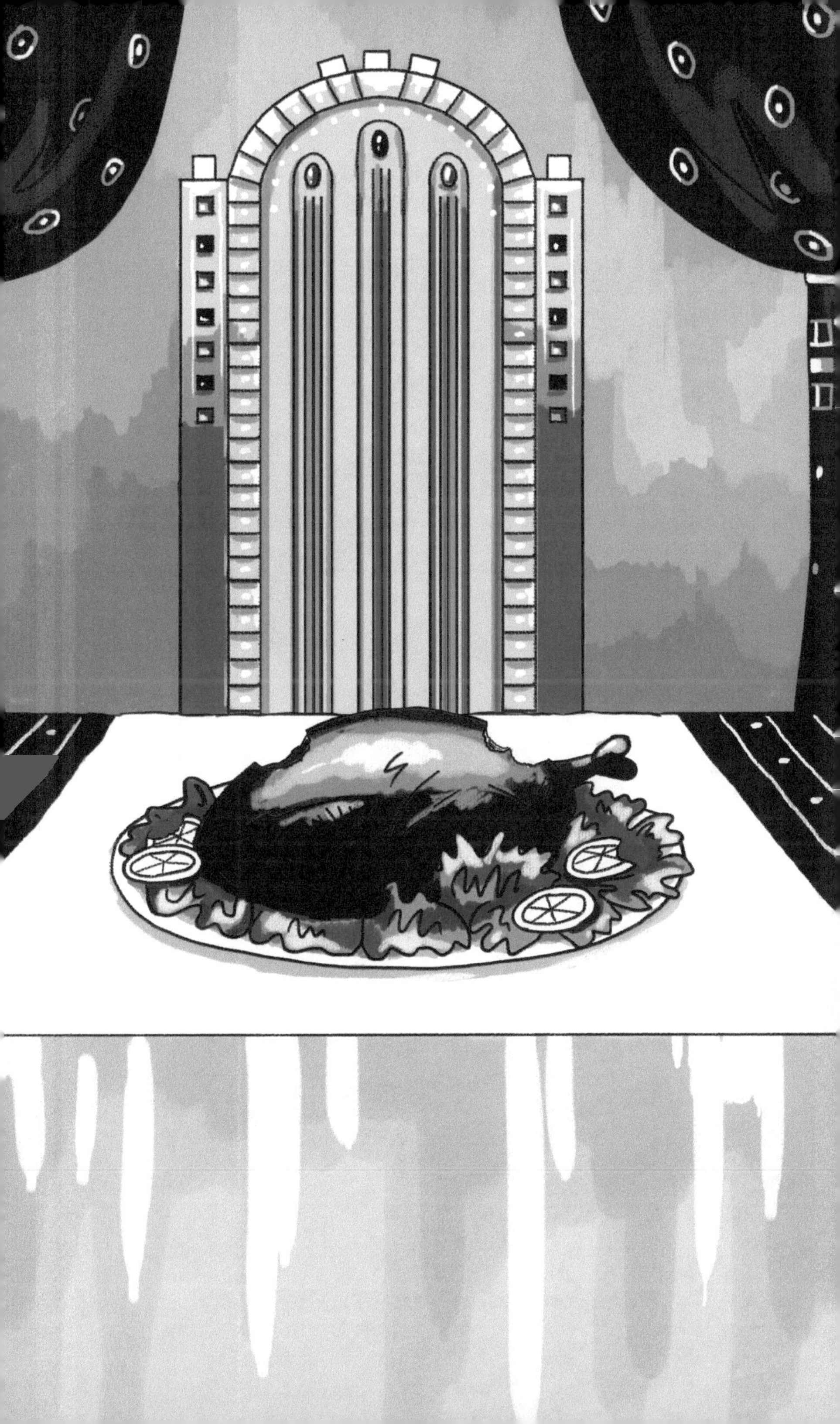

The Dragon from Tarascon

THE DRAGON FROM TARASCON

I

In ancient times there was a giant rock rooted in the deep water of the Rhône where King René built his famous castle. There was a wide cleft in the rock just above the water. It was home to a dragon. The Dragon was so horrible and cruel that the locals were in constant terror of their property and lives.

Nobody could describe what he actually looked like because those who were unlucky enough to encounter him never came back. He would spare neither donkeys nor horses, neither lambs nor children, neither old women nor young girls.

Once misfortune befell a local fisherman. His family and neighbors came to his house to mourn over a poor man's son who had fallen victim to the monster.

A young girl wearing a white festive dress was passing by. She stopped near the fisherman's hut to ask in surprise, "Why are you lamenting?"

"The awful Tarasque has eaten a boy," they replied.

"Who is the Tarasque?"

"The Dragon that lives on the bank of the Rhône. Everybody knows the place but nobody has entered it."

"Alright, I'll pay a visit to him in the morning."

The fishermen gave her a confused look. "He'll gulp you down in no time."

"Well, we'll see," the girl answered. "Could you give me something to eat and a place to sleep? I'll do your laundering tomorrow."

The fishermen did not hesitate to offer shelter to the girl.

II

The following morning, she brought a basket of linen to the foot of the rock and began to wash it. The fishermen hid in the bushes nearby to watch her.

All of a sudden there were bubbles on the water, the ground shook, and wind started to whish in the reeds. The Dragon's monstrous head surfaced, splashing dark waves onto the girl's white dress.

"Who are you?" he roared in a thunderous voice.

"My name is Martha. I'm a stranger here."

"Aren't you afraid of me?"

"Why should I be?"

"Because I'm the Tarasque. Just look how terrible I am! One can't bear the sight of me!"

"I can look at you and still breathe," the girl replied calmly and continued laundering. The Tarasque came closer to her. The fishermen shrank with horror. They regretted encouraging the stranger's reckless attitude.

As the Dragon hung over the girl, she could see that his scales were slimy and covered in dirty seaweed.

"Hey!" the laundress gave him an innocent look and threw a handful of water at him, "You're going to foul the linen!"

The Dragon froze. He was too shocked to speak.

"Poor little thing!" Martha went on in a gentle voice. "Nobody takes care of you. Do sit down and tell me what bothers you. You see, I used to run away in times of trouble to wander on the sea shore all alone..."

Something incredible happened to the Dragon. Tears welled in his red eyes. He got out of the water, sat down next to the girl and asked her, "Please tell me what happened to you there, on the sea shore."

Martha told him her story. She spoke about her home and people whom she met during her trips, about stranger lands and common people, their love and hope. Her voice was so smooth and warm that the horrible Dragon fell asleep at her feet like a kitten.

III

Astonished, the fishermen made a run for the village. Soon all locals came to the river bank. They were stupefied to see the stranger wash slime off the monster's scaled body. Then she took off her belt and put it around his neck to lead him like a pet. The crowd burst into roar, shaking spears and axes.

"Don't!" the girl screamed. "Listen to reason! He won't harm you anymore."

But those who had lost their children and brothers, horses, bulls, and sheep, those who had been living in terror and humiliation could not restrain their hatred. Nobody listened to the stranger. The vengeful crowd fell on the Dragon.

Before he died, the Dragon gave a look of deep gratitude to the girl and said, "You taught me what kindness is. You made me feel like hatred was about to leave my heart. My breath grew clean and my eyes soft... I was about to believe I could be beautiful!"

He collapsed onto the ground to never move again.

Having killed the Dragon, the people indulged in wild songs and dance.

They were too busy celebrating to see Martha leave forever, as unnoticed as she came.

They tell this fairy tale in Provence.

The King's Lace

THE KING'S LACE

I

Once the King wanted to know who could weave the best lace in his kingdom. So he ordered all lace-makers to bring their works to the city hall not later than on the first day of the winter.

Soon there was no single thread left in city shops. One could hear the noise of lace bobbins day and night while lace-makers were working hard to make the best lace they could for the King.

On the skirts of the city, right under the roof of the house, lived little Delphine and her Granny. Granny used to be a wonderful lace-maker. But now she was too old to work. "What shall we do?" Granny sighed. "I'm too old, and we don't have enough money for silk yarn." "What about me?" asked Delphine. "I can! You've taught me everything!" "You little thing," Granny shook her head, "you're too young for such work."

Hearing the bobbin noise as she was walking along the street made Delphine sigh. If only Granny and she could afford fine silk thread! What lace she would make! But the little money that they have was hardly enough to buy bread and cheese.

II

The girl plucked up the courage and asked the Shopkeeper to borrow her some silk thread, but he laughed at her and sent her out. It hurt so much that Delphine burst into tears as soon as she got home.

"Don't you cry, dear," Granny comforted her, "*our day will come!*[1]" "If only I had some thread, Granny, what lace I would make!" "We have no thread, Dear," Granny said with a sigh, "only cobweb in the corners." "Cobweb? What if I use it to make lace?"

Granny shook her head with a smile.

III

Delphine collected a giant ball of cobweb on the following day.

"Please forgive me," she said to the Spider, who lived in the darkest corner.

Of course, the Spider was displeased. But the girl and her Granny never shouted at seeing him or tried to brushed him away. They always gave him some breadcrumbs. So the spider took it easy.

It was a very hard work. Before she could even start making lace, she had to split the cobweb into threads, then twirl it on the bobbins. She had to try over and over again. The Spider was watching Delphine. He liked her perseverance and her wonderful thin lace, which looked as light as a feather.

Only a day before the date, Delphine ran out of cobweb. She rummaged through the attic, went down to the cellar, but found nothing. Disappointed, she fell asleep near her unfinished work.

The Spider felt sorry for the girl. He wanted to help her. The Spider worked for the whole night and did not hide in his dark corner until the dawn.

IV

When Delphine woke up to see her work finished, she said, "I don't know to whom I should say it, but thank you very much!"

The Spider did not say anything. Firstly, he could not speak. Secondly, he was very tired.

---

[1] Notre jour viendra.

The King liked Delphine's work the best. Everyone was asking where she bought such fine yarn. The girl kept telling it was a friend's present. She received the royal award. Granny and she moved to a pretty house, where the Spider still sits in the dark corner just under the roof and makes his lace.

Ball of Wool

BALL OF WOOL

Aunt Miette from Messe village was so very greedy that she would eagerly shear an egg.

Once as she, spinning wheel in hand, was driving her cows to the field, she found a ball of wool on the road. It looked like a little animal. She bent down for it. She was in such a hurry that she did not even think about the spinner who had lost the ball. She could almost see it in the large pocket of her apron, which seemed to be meant for it.

But Aunt Miette could not get the ball. It rolled on and on, so she had to leave her spinning wheel by the road.

Now her hands were free and stretching out to catch the ball. But it kept rolling on and on! Aunt Miette forgot about her spinning wheel and her wonderful cows, who took the usual way to the pasture. She was chasing the ball, which kept escaping her hands.

Short of breath, she crossed the meadow and climbed a hill without even noticing it. It seemed like she would run to the end of the earth to get it.

At long last, she caught the end of the thread.

She began to wrap it around her fingers until she had a wonderful ball of wool, while the bigger one did not get any smaller and rolled on, followed by old Miette.

She was content to hold the thread as her ball was growing. She could make a jacket and a pair of trousers for her husband, a skirt for herself, and sell the rest of the wool... Lucky Aunt Miette! She was tireless.

The ball soon grew too large to wrap the thread around it. Aunt Miette was very disappointed but had to tear it with a sad sigh.

All of a sudden, the ball that she had been chasing vanished in a single leap. The one in her hands followed it that very moment though she was holding it tight.

The old lady had to chase it again! She caught the end of the thread. She made a ball twenty times, and all in vain.

Aunt Miette was seen all around the province that day. Her hair disheveled, short of breath, tired, she still kept chasing the ball and winding the thread.

He husband found the two cows in the field and his wife's spinning wheel by the road. Old Miette has been running through woods and fields since then because she cannot stop.

If you find a ball of wool on the road, please pick it up just to return it to the one who lost it.

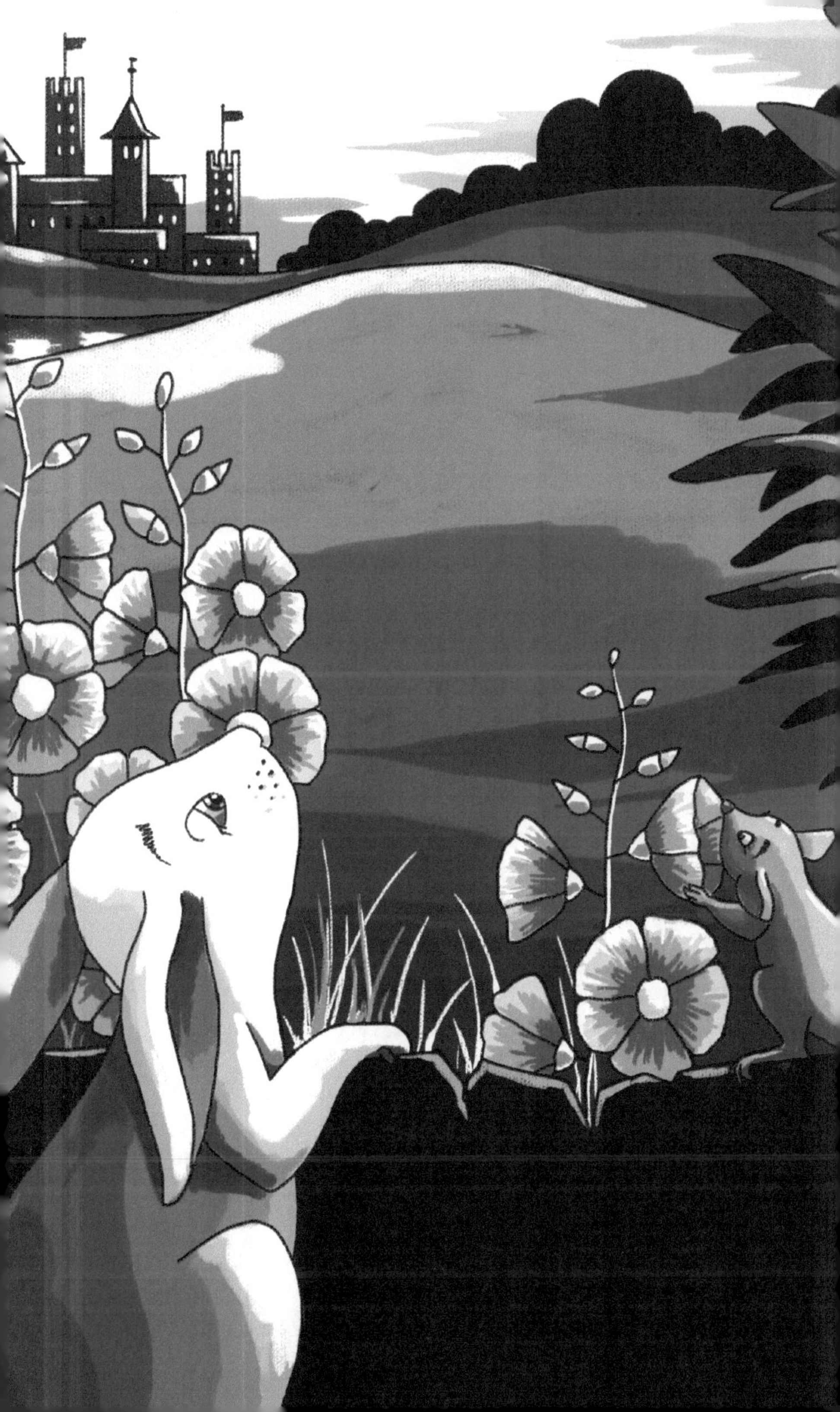

Why the Rabbit Does Not Talk

WHY THE RABBIT DOES NOT TALK

Once a man had a Cock and a Rabbit. He assigned duties to each of them. The Cock was to crow every morning to wake up the family. The Rabbit was expected to produce a lot of warm down to make boots and coats of. They were good workers and received a lot of praise and food from their owner.

But once it occurred to the Rabbit, "The man says thank you to the Cock for waking up the family every day. Even our neighbors can hear him crow. But I'm forgotten for the rest of the year as soon as they take my down."

The Rabbit spoke to the Cock, "You have such a nice voice, Friend. Everybody can hear it. You enjoy admiration and praise. Please teach me to crow too. We'll wake up our owner and neighbors together."

The Cock hesitated for a while before saying, "Alright, I'll teach you to crow. Please mind that it's not easy. You'll have to work hard every day until your throat is as strong as mine and you can crow that loudly."

The two of them agreed.

The Cock woke up the Rabbit early on the following morning.

"Repeat it," he said, "but don't hurry. *Good and quickly seldom meet.*[1]" Having said so, he stretched his neck.

The Rabbit would not wait until his throat was as strong as that of the Cock. He drew a deep breath and screamed at the top of his lungs. He woke up nobody but lost his voice.

This is why the Rabbit is the only domestic animal who doesn't talk.

[1] Vite et bien se trouvent rarement ensemble.

The Large Stove

THE LARGE STOVE

A man had a big pretty house, the best house in the whole town. He was very proud of it because it had cost him a lot.

The large stove was a highlight because the man couldn't stand cold, and the winter was freezing in that region.

Many rooms in the house were vacant because the man had a small family of himself and his wife. They were childless.

When winter came, the cold wind was piercing. Windows were frosted. The man began to burn wood in the stove. It consumed a lot to heat the empty cold rooms. The man's firewood only lasted a month. When he ran out of it, the spouses began to shiver and chatter their teeth with cold.

The man could not but break his pretty wooden outbuildings for firewood. When it was all burned, the cold became even more bitter, and he still had nothing to stoke the stove with. So the man climbed the roof and broke it into firewood. The house became even colder when it was out. The man had to break his ceiling for more. Seeing him do it, his neighbor asked in surprise, "What are you doing, Neighbor? Are you mad? To break your ceiling open in winter! The two of you will freeze!"

The man replied, "I'm actually breaking the ceiling to stoke my stove and warm up a little. Our stove is special—the more firewood I feed to it, the colder it becomes."

The neighbor said laughingly, "Are you going to break your house when the ceiling's out? You'll have nothing but the cold stove left."

"I must have bad luck. All people have enough firewood for the winter, while I have to burn half the house."

The neighbor said, "You need to remake the stove. *It's as clear as day.*[1]"

The man replied, "I know that you envy me my house and my stove because it's larger than yours. That's why you want me to remake it."

He burned the whole of the ceiling and the house itself, so the family had to take shelter elsewhere. As the saying goes, *to teach a fool is the same as to cure a dead man*[2].

---

[1] Claire comme le jour.
[2] A laver la tête d`un âne on perd la lessive.

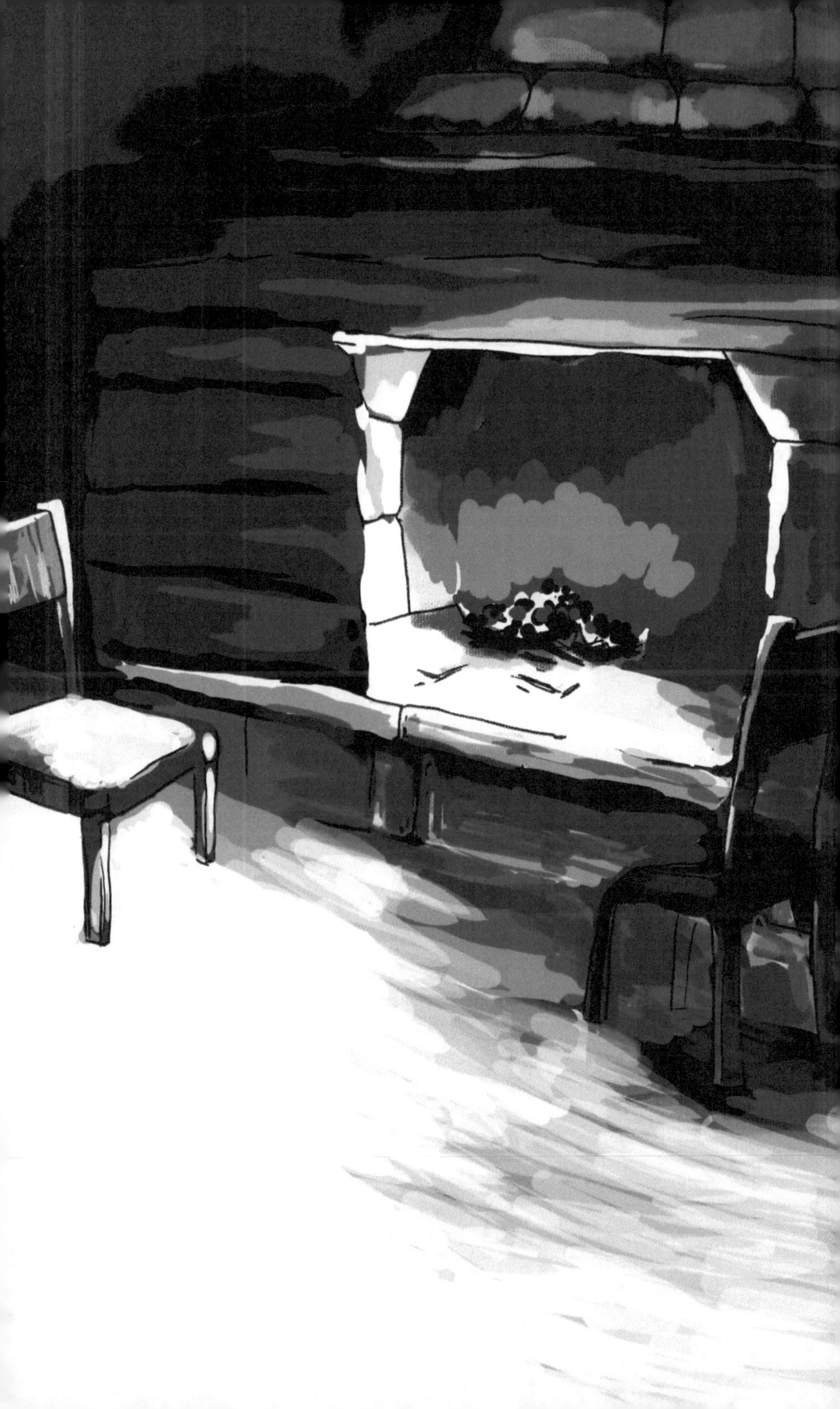

The Lost Compote

THE LOST COMPOTE

Once a Son-in-Law visited his Mother-in-Law. She treated him to steaming soup and hot pie.

"Help yourself, dear Son-in-Law. *Good things in abundance do no harm,*[1]" she said.

She served freshly made compote for dessert.

The Son-in-Law had never tasted anything of the kind, so he asked, "What is this?"

"This is compote, my dear Son-in-Law."

The Son-in-Law liked the compote a lot. He thought, "I should make my wife cook it when at home. If only I could remember the name."

He said thank you and departed.

On his way home, he kept repeating, "Compote! Compote! Compote! I have to remember the name."

It was pitch dark. The poor man failed to notice a ditch and fell down. He hurt his head badly. When he got up, he could not remember the delicious dish that he tried at his Mother-in-Law's. He got headache thinking of it to no avail. He stayed in the ditch until morning because he was too busy thinking.

As a man was passing by on horseback, he saw the Son-in-Law walking in the ditch. He stopped to ask him, "What have you lost in the ditch?"

"A hundred francs," he replied.

"Oh dear! Let me help you," the rider said. "We'll share the money if we find them, alright?"

He got off the horse and said, nearing the ditch, "What a mess! Looks like stodgy compote!"

"I've found it!" the Son-in-Law screamed with joy. He leaped out of the ditch, jumped onto the man's horse, and galloped home, shouting, "Compote! Compote!"

[1] Abondance de biens ne nuit pas.

Three Artful Sons

THREE ARTFUL SONS

Once upon a time, a poor man had three sons. When they grew up, their father told them, "You should learn a trade. Your life will be hard if you have no skills."

So they left. When they came home, they said, "We are skillful now, so we can earn a living."

The father was glad to see his sons and wanted to give them a treat. He started to fry eggs. The eldest son said to him, "You don't have to do this, Dad. I'm a cook now, so I can fry the eggs for you. Please wait at the gate."

The eldest son used vine leaves to make a strong fire. When the eggs were ready, he smashed his fist on the pan handle, sending the eggs through the chimney right onto his father's plate.

The father was delighted at how artful he was.

When the four of them sat down to the table, a horseman stopped at the gate. He wanted his horse shoed.

"It's my trade," the middle son said, "because I'm a smith."

He took a horseshoe, put it into fire, and said to the horseman, "Please pace back a little and then gallop to the gate as fast as you can."

The horseman darted to the gate. The middle son threw the horseshoe so artfully that it landed right on the horse's hoof.

The father was delighted by how artful he was.

All of a sudden, it began to hail. The father feared lest it should damage his crops.

The youngest son said, "Now it's my turn to show my skills."

He grabbed a stick and started to combat the hail. He broke each single pellet of ice before it could hit the crops.

The father was really happy to see his sons so skillful.

P.S.
People tell the tale in a different way nowadays.

They say, the eldest son learned programming and made sure that all household devices, from the fridge to the laptop, worked forever and never upset their owners.

The middle son became a policeman and put an end to any thefts.

The youngest son became a doctor. He prevented every citizen from ever falling ill.

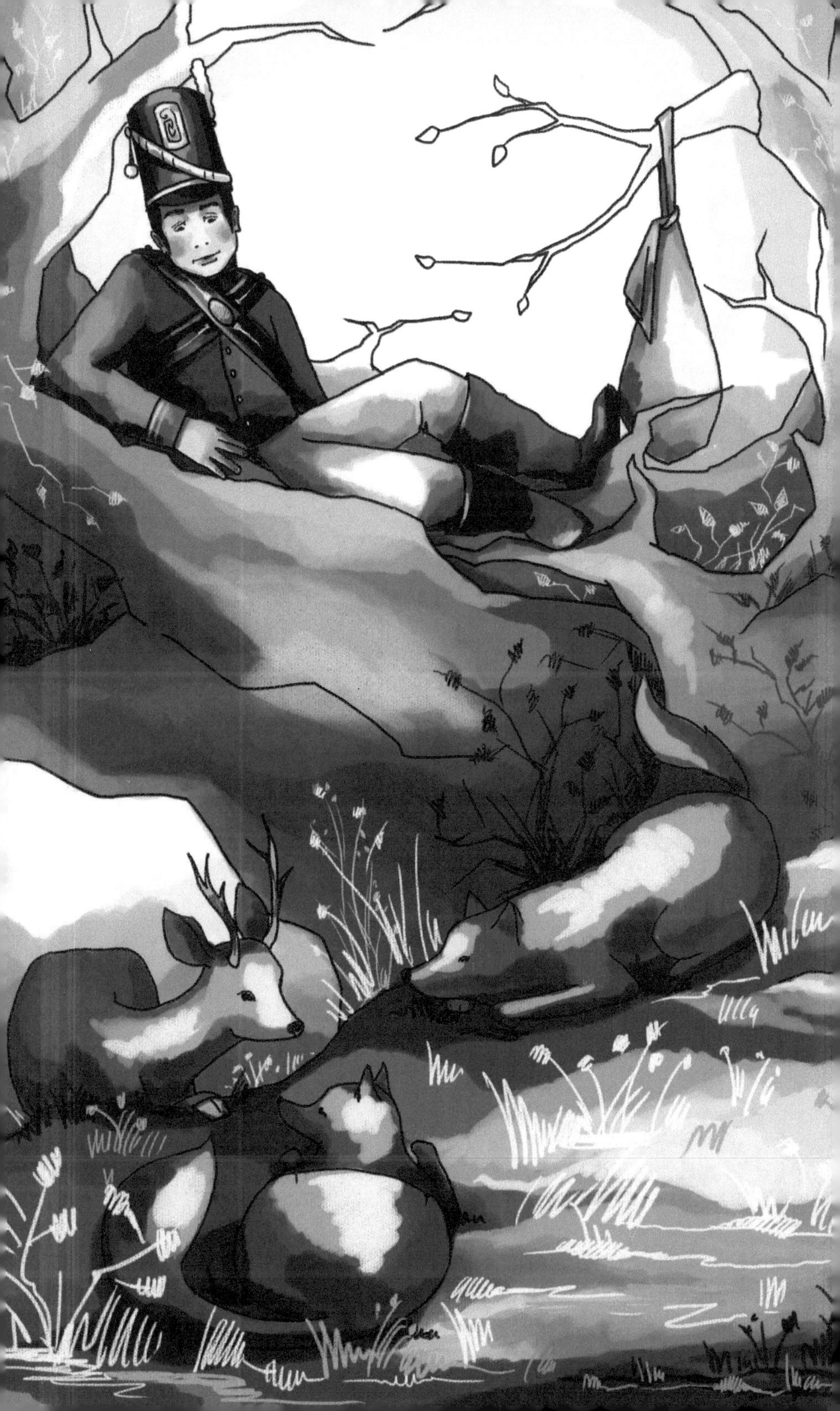

The Careless Wife

THE CARELESS WIFE

Once upon a time there lived a Husband and Wife. The Husband loved his Wife dearly because she was the most beautiful woman in the village. She was very lazy and careless. She would not do any housework like cooking, feeding the hens, or gardening. The beautiful Wife spent her days admiring her image in the mirror. Besides, she was a hearty eater and spent all their money for nuts and cakes. Finally, she had nothing but a torn shirt left.

When a big holiday came, the Wife had nothing to wear but for the shirt. So she said to her husband, "Will you go to the market and buy the prettiest shirt you can find for me, dear Hubby?"

The Husband scratched his head. He knew that it would be wrong to spend their last money for clothes. But he could not stand to deny his Wife's request. *What the woman wants, God wants*[1]. The husband went to the market. He was looking for a shirt when he saw a goose.

"A holiday without a treat is no holiday at all! We'd rather wear torn shirts than have nothing to eat!" thought the Husband and bought the goose instead of a shirt.

When he came home, the Wife asked him, "Have you bought a shirt for me?"

"I've bought something—a **goose**," he replied.

The Wife misheard it. "I don't mind its being a little bit too **loose**," she said.

She hurried to take off the torn shirt and threw it into the fire. "Where's the new one? I want to wear it right now!" she demanded.

"I told you I'd bought a goose and not a shirt!" the Husband replied.

The beautiful Wife had not a single shirt to wear.

As the saying goes, *make haste slowly*[2].

---
[1] Que Femme veut — dieu le veut.
[2] Hâte-toi lentement!

The Chetty Tree

THE CHERRY TREE

Many birds lived in a garden. Each of them was proud of their coat or voice. Only the old Thrush neither had pretty feathers nor could sing well. Once, the birds decided that the Thrush did not belong in the beautiful garden because he had a dull coat and a hoarse voice, which people didn't like. The Thrush had to leave the garden and get settled on an old cherry tree in the woods. He could only see his ex-friends and hear them sing from a distance. He felt very sad and lonely.

The Thrush spent the summer picking cherries and hiding them in a tree hollow, preparing for a cold winter. Summer was over. Fall came. Many birds from the garden flew away to the south. Those who stayed quarreled over each single berry or nut.

Winter came. The Thrush could hear other birds sing very rarely now. Once he came to the garden. He could hardly find several frozen, starved birds. People, who had been admiring their voices and coats, had not left them anything to eat. The birds were dying of hunger.

"Come along," said the Thrush. "I have some food. We can stand the cold together."

The birds were so weak that they could hardly move their wings. But they began to feel better after they tasted some dried cherries in the warm hollow.

"Please forgive us, Thrush," they said, "*a friend in need is a friend indeed.*[1]"

Birds did not chirp in the garden that spring. It was empty and quiet. The best singers showed off their bright feathers on the old cherry tree in the woods.

[1] Au besoin on connaît l'ami.

Two Old Soldiers

TWO OLD SOLDIERS

I

Once two old soldiers were returning home. They both had been injured. One was blind; the other had a less severe injury. They went begging from house to house. People were generous to them. But the blind one hardly benefited from it because his guide would have all tasty things and leave him nothing but bones and stale bread.

The miserable man said, "I am so unhappy. Why hurt me?"

"I'll leave you alone if you keep complaining," the second soldier replied.

This could not keep the poor blind man from complaining. His guide eventually left him in a forest.

II

The blind man wandered about for some time before he stopped near a tree to think. "What will happen to me? Wild animals will tear me to pieces when night comes."

He decided to climb the tree so that animals could not get him.

At about midnight, the Fox, the Wolf, and the Deer came.

The Fox was the first to speak.

"There is a river not far away from here which makes blind people see. I have got bling in an eye many times. The water's never failed to cure me. I only have to wash myself with it."

"I know the river," the Wolf said. "I know it even better than you do. The King's daughter is very ill. They promise to marry her off to the one who cures her. She'll get better as soon as she drinks some water from the river."

The Deer said, "The city of Lyon suffers from water shortage. They promise a huge reward to the one who helps it. It you dig the ground near the Tree of Liberty, it will reveal a spring, and they'll have enough water."

The animals left.

"I wish I could find the river!" said the blind man.

III

In the morning, he got off the tree and felt his way through the woods. At last, he reached the river. When he rinsed his eyes, he could see something. He rinsed them again, and his sight became really sharp.

Then the soldier hurried to meet the Mayor of Lyon and recommend him to dig the ground near the Tree of Liberty. Indeed, they found a spring, and the city had plenty of water. Having received the reward, the soldier went to see the King.

"Your Majesty," he said, "I know your daughter to be badly ill. But I know the cure." And he told him about the water.

The King did not hesitate to send his servants to the river. They gave some water to the Princess and washed her in it. She got better at once.

The King told the soldier, "Even though you are a common soldier, you can marry my daughter if you want to."

The soldier agreed, and they had a wedding on the same day.

Once when the soldier was walking in his garden, he saw a beggar. He recognized him to be his old friend. He came up to the beggar and gave him generous alms. He held no grudge for him.

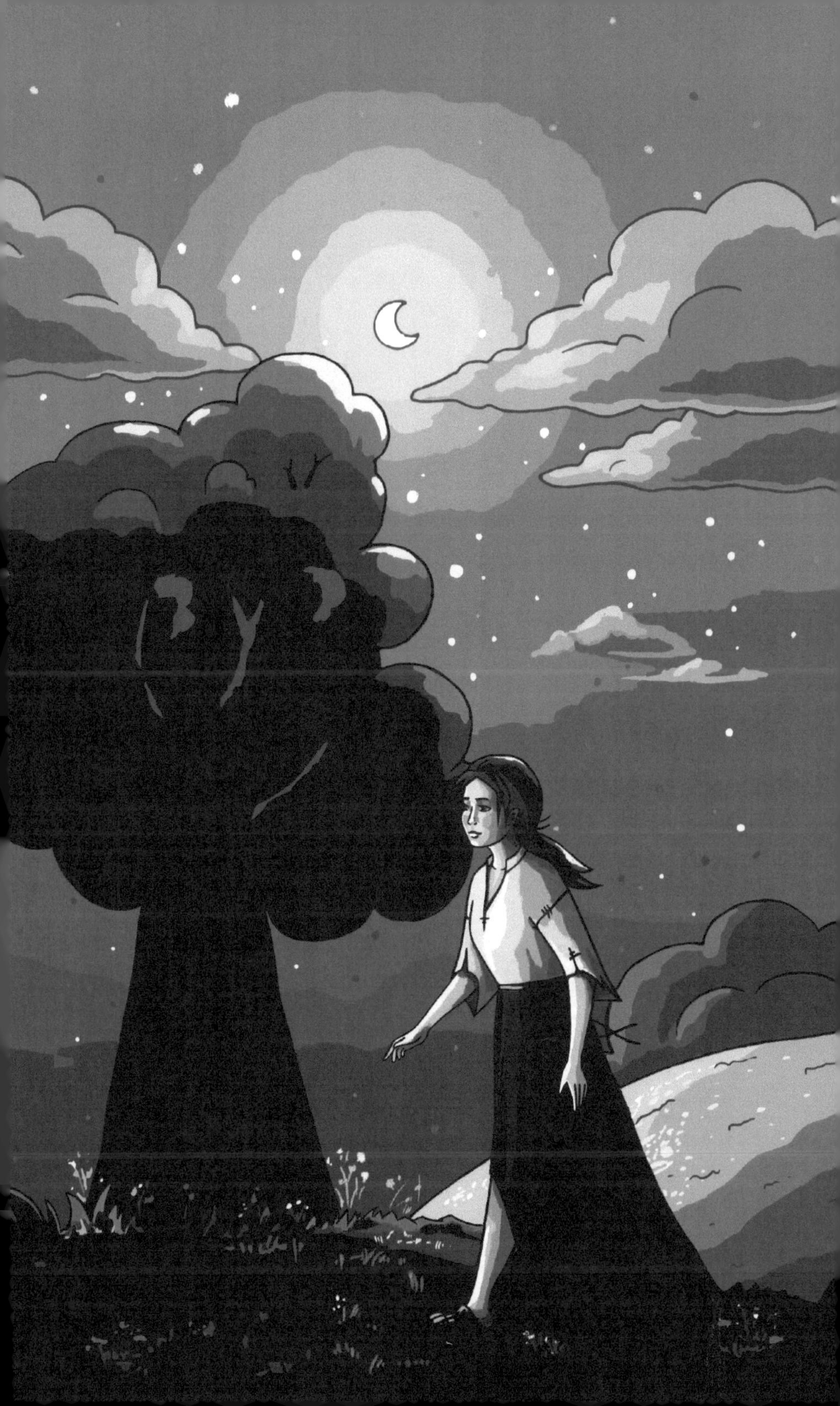

Bernique! Bernique!

BERNIQUE! BERNAQUE!

Once a poor man ordered a pair of boots from the shoemaker. He did not pay for a long time. The shoemaker was tired of reminding the poor man about his debt, so he said, "Listen, poor man. I could help you repay your debt."

"Why, I'd like you to!"

"Let's agree like this. From now on you must keep silent and answer all questions with two words, "Bernique! Bernaque!" That's it. Don't speak until I allow you to. Got it?"

"Sure. I'll just keep saying, "Bernique! Bernaque!" The poor man nodded his head contentedly and went home.

When he came, his wife began to grumble, "Where have you been?"

"Bernique!" her husband replied humbly.

"What?" she asked in a surprised voice.

"Bernaque!"

"Dear! What's the matter with you?"

She heard nothing but "Bernique! Bernaque!" What could she do? She decided to see the judge. He was thought to be a wise man and could probably help her husband.

So she hurried to the judge.

"Please come to our home, will you? My husband's mad!"

"Is he? I don't think so," the judge said hesitantly.

"Can a person who only says "Bernique! Bernaque!" be sane?"

"I see... I know the word that will heal him." The judge was a little boastful. "It will cost ten coins," he added because he loved money even more than he loved fame.

The poor woman agreed with a sigh. The judge came to the poor man's house and said, "God help you, poor man!"

"Bernique!" the poor man replied.

"What are you mumbling?"

"Bernaque!" the poor man replied.

The judge tried hard but failed to make the poor man say anything but the two words.

Once the judge encountered the shoemaker.

"Hello, Mr. Judge," the shoemaker said with a bow.

"Hello."

"What's the parish news, Mr. Judge?"

"I think you already know our poor man to be mad, don't you?"

"Ha, ha! The poor man is no less sane than me or you!"

"Don't you be foolish."

"I'm not. He's perfectly sane."

"Don't you argue with me! I bet the poor man's mad!"

"I put ten coins on this. He's not."

"Let it be fifty," the judge could not resist it.

"Deal!"

The two of them went to the poor man at once. The shoemaker said, "Hi there." And he whispered to the poor man, "You may speak now."

The poor man sighed with relief. "It's been a long time since I last saw you. I think my boots have cost me far too much."

"Forget it. You'd better ask our greedy judge how much it has cost *him*."

The judge got red in his face. He threw fifty coins onto the table and left without saying goodbye.

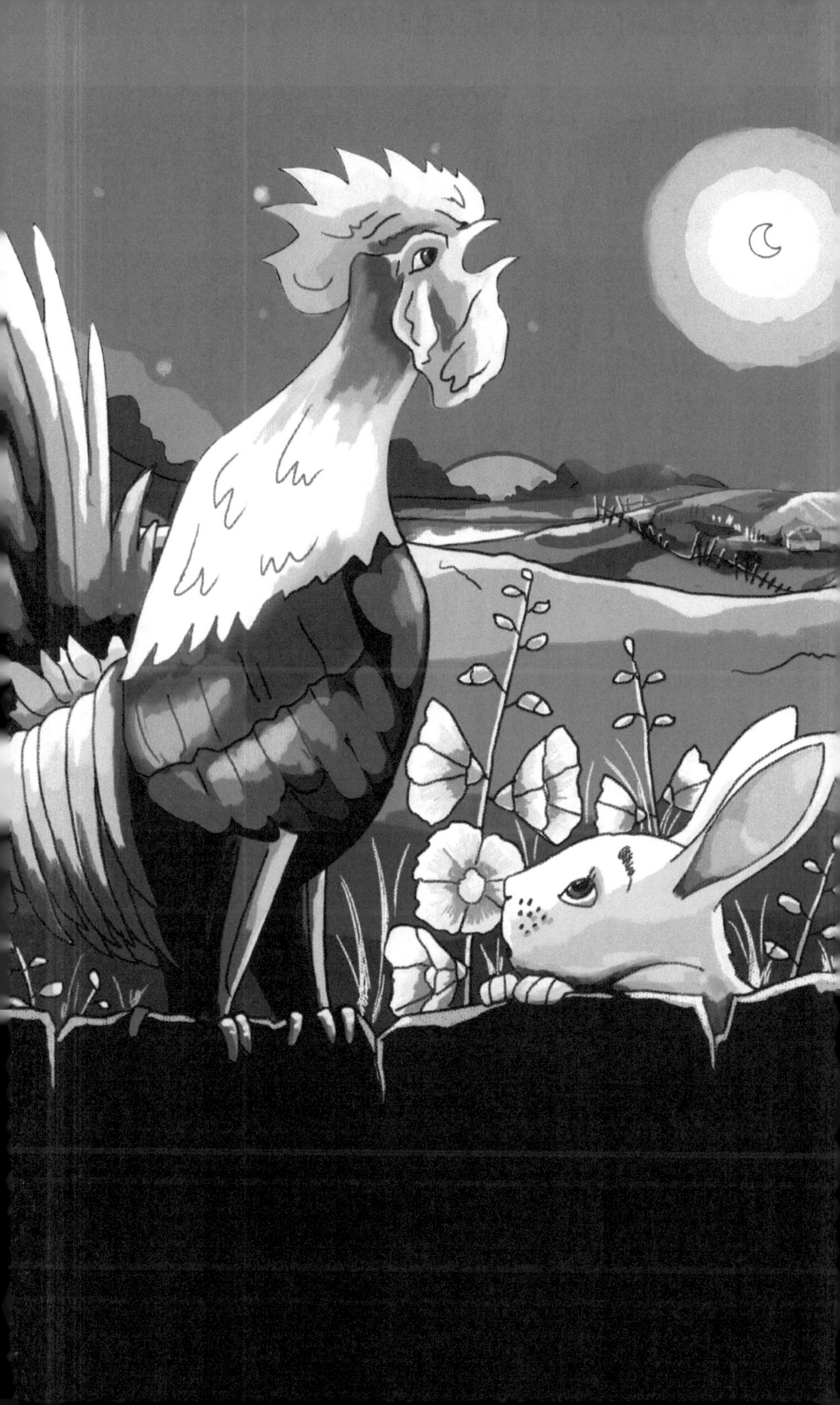

How the Moon Fell in Love with the Sun

HOW THE MOON FELL IN LOVE WITH THE SUN

Many thousands of centuries ago, the Sun and the Moon ruled the world alternately.

The Sun was the king of the day and the ruler over all day birds and animals. He ordered flowers to bloom, insects to wake up, and everything to buzz with life.

When the day neared its end and the Sun's time was over, he would set to sleep comfortably in high hills. As soon as the last ray of sunlight faded, the Moon would take over the Sun. She would rise gracefully from behind the trees, pouring its silver shine onto them. When in the dark sky, the Moon would open her eyes. At that very moment everything was ornamented with a silver lace of shadows. Nature fell asleep. Life slowed down. The Moon admired the silent world.

As the day came again, the Sun would take over the Moon. They went on like this until one day.

Once the Sun was too slow. He failed to set on time. The Moon woke up and rose to the sky. The soft touch of warm rays made her open her eyes to see the radiant golden Sun. It was love at first sight. However, the Sun hid in the high hills before she knew it, taking along the last ray of light.

The Moon hurried to rise like never before in the following night because she wanted to catch a glimpse of her beloved one. However, she could not see him no matter how hard she tried.

"*Day by day, I love you more than I did yesterday but less than I will tomorrow,*[1]" the Moon would sing

---

[1] Chaque jour je t'aime davantage, aujourd'hui plus qu'hier mais moins que demain.

at night. But there was nobody to hear her because the Earth was sound asleep.

Once, the Moon could not stand it anymore. She cried bitterly, scattering silver tears across the dark sky. They shone brightly.

Since then her tears have lit up in the sky, one by one, as soon as the Moon rises. We know them as stars.

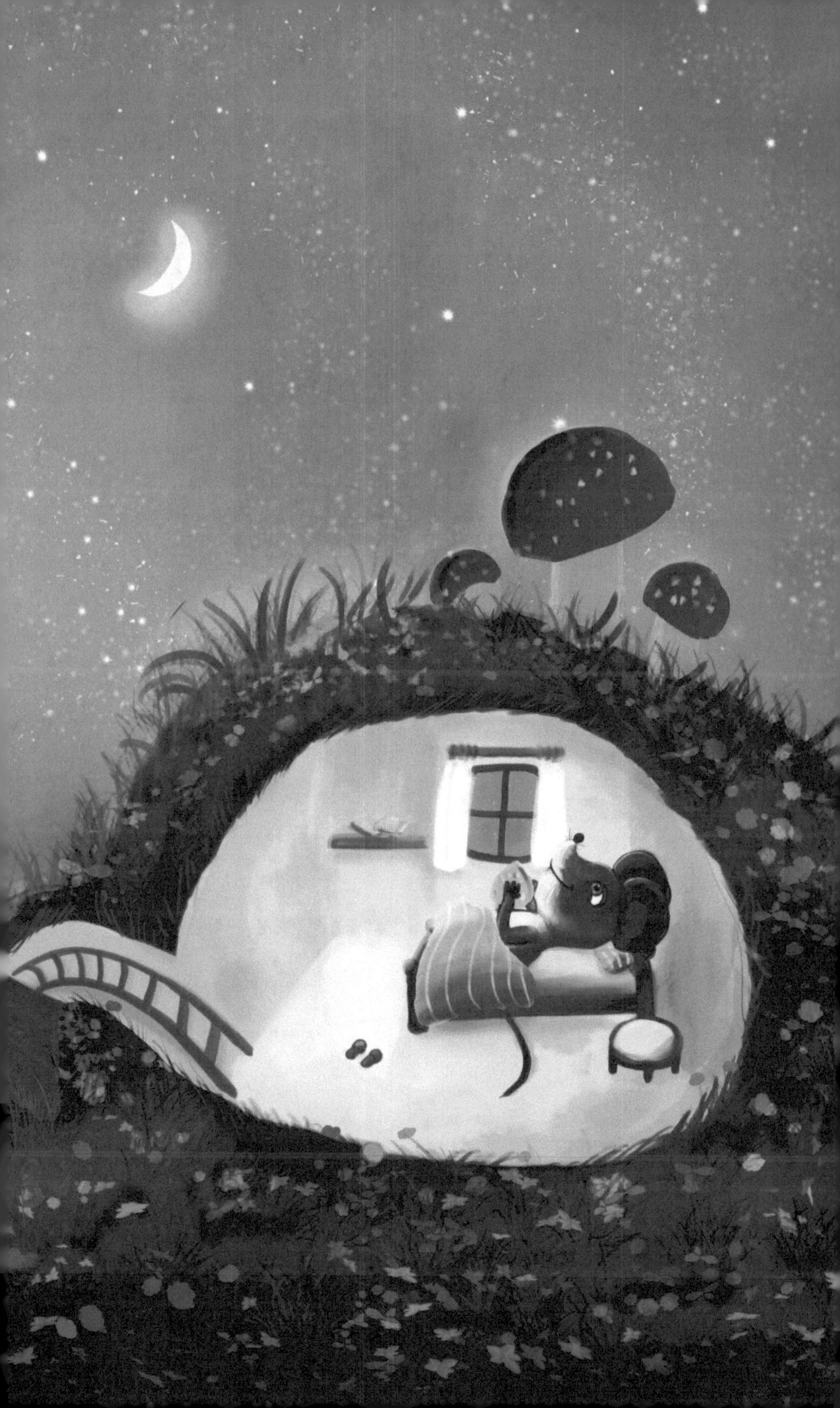

The Boys of Mayenne

THE BOYS OF MAYENNE

Once upon a time, two boys from the village of Mayenne were walking down the road. They found three gold coins. Lucky them!

But how should they divide them? There were only two boys for three coins!

They scratched their heads to no avail. Then they decided to play a counting game. "One. It's mine!" "Two. It's yours!" Whose is the third one? It was no good.

"You and me is two." "Me and you is three." What happened to one? This failed too.

The boys of Mayenne decided to ask Uncle Jacques.

Uncle Jacques did not hesitate to give a coin to one of the boys, another to the second one, and keep the third one. Smart, isn't it?

Uncle Jacques has a head of gold!

Or rather a chest of it. They call him Chest of Gold in the village.

Why do you think?

The Dog and the Moon

THE DOG AND THE MOON

Once upon a time, the Dog found a large bone. He had long been hungry, so he did not want to share it. He spent the day looking for a nice place for dinner, where nobody would disturb him.

At last, the Dog sat down on the bank of a lake. He was about to taste the bone when the golden full moon rose, pouring beautiful light all around. The water was still in the lake, showing a reflection on the moon.

The Dog mistook it for a fatty pancake. He did not hesitate to give up his bone and jump at the moon. It sunk, stirring the water.

The Dog came out disappointed. When the water grew still, it reflected the shiny yellow pancake again. The Dog leaped at the moon again but to no avail. The noise that he made attracted other animals. They took the bone while the Dog was trying to catch the moon and made fun of him.

The Dog looked at the sky and saw the same golden pancake, only much higher and brighter. He realized that he had given up his bone for nothing.

He grew angry with the moon for leaving him hungry and ridiculous. This is why dogs bark and howl at the moon when it is full.

An Incident in the Bois de Boulogne

An Incident In The Bois De Boulogne

In the oldest oak tree in the Bois de Boulogne there lived a sparrow named Agile and his family. He was the youngest of all nestlings, the most mischievous of all. Agile often got in trouble, and his brothers and sisters had to help him out every time.

This is what happened. When his parents and elder siblings flew away to get some food, Agile decided to see what was going on down there. He spent most of his time in the nest, which lay high on an oak branch. Of course, he wanted to know who lived on the ground.

As he was trying to fly off the tree, Agile's wing caught on the branches. He found himself hanging in the air. He could not get down on his own, so he began to call for help. The Pigeon was passing by and shouted, "Try using your beak!" But it was no use.

The Crown croaked from a near tree, "Move your wings!" But her advice did not help the poor sparrow.

Agile's wing was stuck tight in the branches. Tiny teardrops began to fall from his eyes. He was tired. The wing hurt him badly.

All of a sudden, something wet and slippery fell onto the tree from above, hitting Agile on his little head. The blow released his wing, and the sparrow shot up into the sky. He was happy to feel free. As he glanced down, he saw a fish, who fell into the lake and disappeared. Only her silvery tail sparkled. It was the fish who set Agile free! But do fishes fall down from the sky?

"Bad luck!" the Seagull complained in the sky, "to drop such a fish! I shouldn't have listened to the Crown and the Pigeon!"

Agile the Sparrow was already comfortable in the nest, cleaning his feathers. *A misfortune can sometimes help.*[1]

---
[1] À quelque chose malheur est bon.

The Bird Named It's Mine

THE BIRD NAMED IT'S MINE

Once upon a time, there lived a tiny Bird with a huge voice. Everybody across the forest could hear it when she sang.

The little Bird had a taste for sweet fruit and berries. When she chanced to find something of the kind, she would scream, "It's mine! It's mine!" This is why other animals called her It's Mine.

Once as she was flying in the forest, the Bird could smell something sweet and delicious. She followed the smell until she saw a tall tree with something hidden among its thick leaves. When she came closer, she saw something really miraculous. The Bird had never seen such ripe and juicy fruits. They were so many that they could last her for a year or more.

The Bird was afraid lest other birds find the tree, so she screamed, "It's mine! It's mine!" She screamed at the top of her lungs, attracting all the birds in the forest. They saw the ripe fruits and devoured them before the Bird knew it.

This is what greed can result in when untamed.

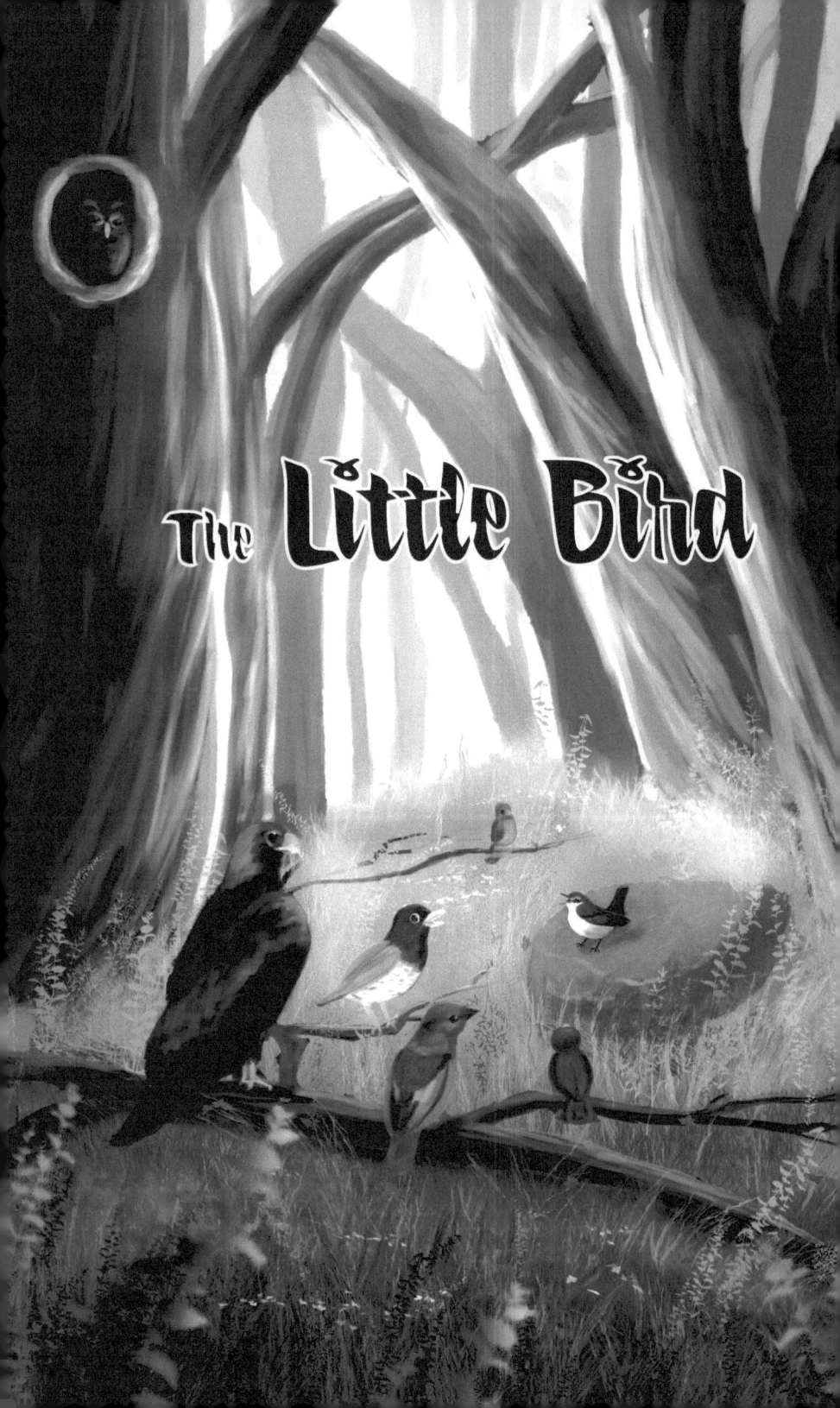

The Little Bird

THE LITTLE BIRD

Once a very long time ago, there was no fire in the world, and nobody knew how to get it. Then the decision was taken to go to God and fetch some fire.

But God is far away. Who could reach him? They turned to large birds. Large birds refused; so did smaller ones. Even the Skylark would not do it.

Hearing them argue, the Little Bird said, "I'll go there if nobody wants to!" "But your body is so small! Your wings are so short! You'll die of fatigue before you even get there." "I'll try," said the Little Bird. "If I die on my way, then so be it."

So she set off and flew so fast that she soon reached the throne of God. He was very surprised to see her. He put her on his lap but hesitated to give her fire. "You'll burn before you reach the ground."

But the Little Bird insisted.

"Alright. I'll give you what you ask for." God said. "But don't hurry. If you fly too fast, your feathers will catch fire."

The Little Bird promised to be careful. She flew off for the land merrily. She remembered the advice and did not hurry at first. But when she saw everyone waiting for her on the ground, she could not resist flying faster.

What God had predicted happened. She brought fire to the ground. Everyone got hold of it at once. Every single feather of the poor little bird had burned down!

All birds began to bustle around her. Each tore a feather of hers to make a dress for the little bird. Now she had a colorful coat.

Only the mean Owl would not give her anything. Then all birds attacked the Owl to punish her for being so cruel. The Owl had to hide. This is why she only comes out at night. If she happens to appear in the daytime, all birds attack her at once and force her back into the tree hole.

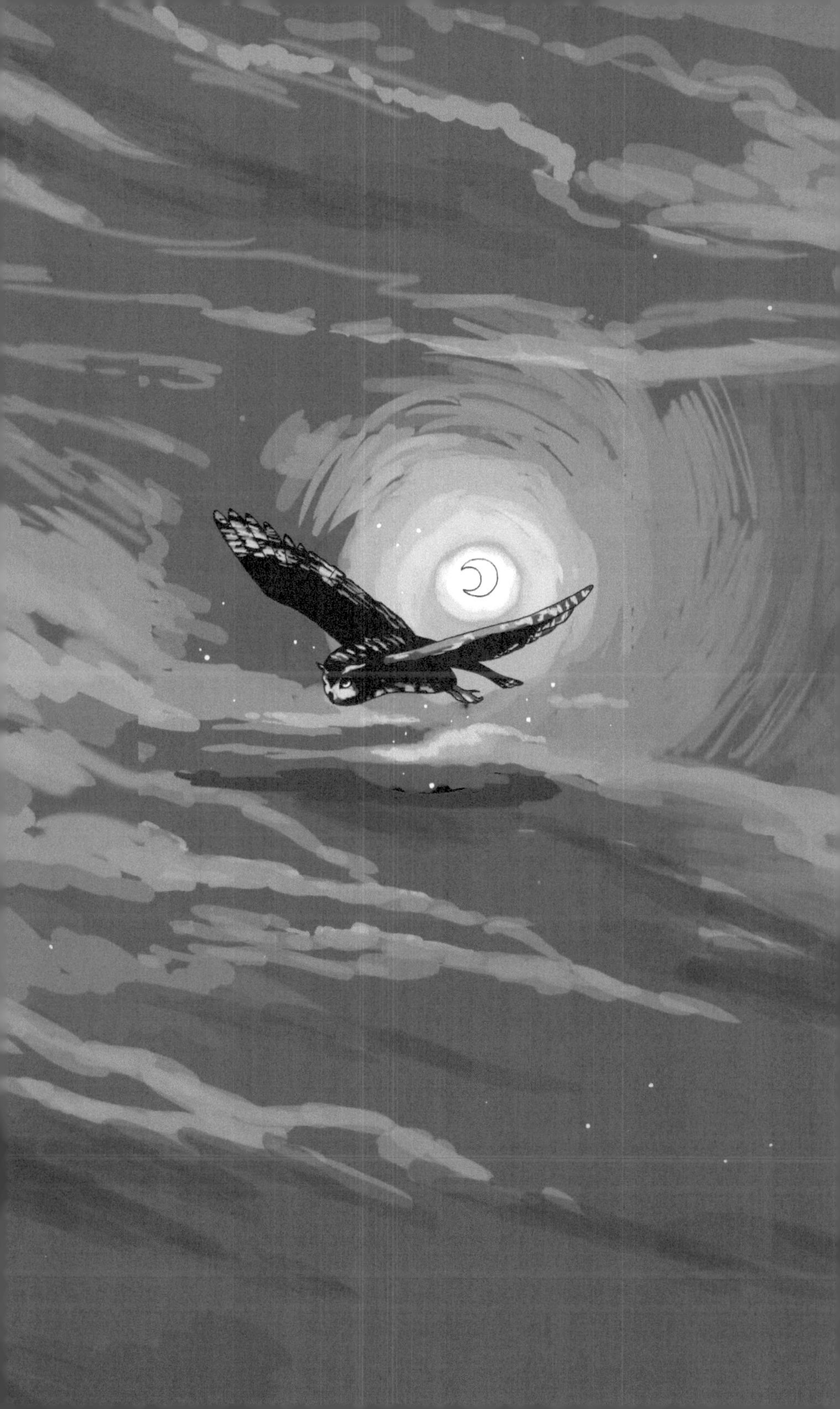

The Eagle and the Cock

THE EAGLE AND THE COCK

The Eagle and the Cock used to be best friends back in the old days. The Cock's wings were long and strong, and he could fly as high as the Eagle. All birds in the world believed them to be the most beautiful and powerful ones.

One day, all birds gathered to elect their king. They disputed all the day long on which of them fitted the high position. They were naturally of equal power and might. Neither was inferior to the other in any way. However, two kings cannot rule one country.

Finally, the birds grew tired of arguing, so the Eagle and the Cock promised to settle it between themselves.

They called at an inn and had a nice meal. They realized that they had nothing to pay with when they were about to leave.

The Eagle suggested to the Cock, "Stay here, Friend. I'll fetch the money and be back in no time."

"Alright," the Cock agreed. "But be quick, or I'll get angry. If you hear me crow three times, you'll know I'm becoming angry."

The Eagle flew out of the window and disappeared in clouds. In fact, he was not going to ever come back because he wanted to be the ruler over all birds.

The Cock waited for a long time. At dawn, he began to get angry. He crowed once, then again, then for a third time. The Eagle never came back.

This is how the Eagle became the ruler over all birds. He became even mightier and stronger, while his friend Cock came to live with people. He has been crowing three times for the Eagle every morning since then.

You never know what will happen next.

That's life.[1]

---

[1] C'est la vie.

The Maid and the Princess

THE MAID AND THE PRINCESS

Once upon a time there lived a princess who had a maid.

The maid would look in the mirror every day, thinking, "I'm no less pretty than the Princess is. My curls are tight. My skin is even whiter than hers and my eyes brighter!" The thoughts always distracted her from her work, and she did not care to do it well. The Maid would get scolded and punished, but that made her envy the Princess even worse.

Once the Prince of a nearby kingdom proposed to the Princess. He sent her a portrait of himself. The Maid became even angrier at seeing it. "Why does the Princess always get the best things?!" she cried and stamped her feet.

The Princess was smiling and preparing to meet her fiancé. Royal tailors had made her a wonderful, beautifully embroidered dress.

"This dress suits me better than her!" the Maid hissed angrily at seeing it through the keyhole.

Having found out which road the Prince was going to come, the Maid decided to steal the dress and meet the Prince herself. She sneaked into the Princess's room at night, took the dress and smeared the rest with paint.

Early in the morning, when everyone was asleep, the Maid left the palace to meet the Prince. She was in such a hurry that she did not watch her steps. She fell many times.

The Prince was shocked to hear a girl wearing a dirty, torn expensive dress, her face also dirty, say that she was the Princess and that he had to marry her. "Just look at my dress!" she screamed. "Only the Princess can wear it! You must marry me now!"

The Prince ordered his people to put the stranger into the carriage and went on.

The Princess was crying bitterly—all of her gowns were ruined. "How can I meet my fiancé?" she sobbed.

Every waiting lady was eager to give her dress to the Princess, but all the garments were either too large or too small.

Only the washerwoman's dress fit the Princess. It was very simple. White collar and cuffs were its only decoration.

When the Prince entered the bailey of the castle, the Maid began to scream again, "It's me whom he should marry! Look at me! Look at my dress! The Prince must be stupid and blind because he can't see the real Princess!"

The Prince was not listening to her. He was looking with a smile at the neat, modest girl wearing a clean dress, who said hello politely.

They locked the jealous Maid in the lumber room because *politeness and neatness are better than dirty beauty.*[1]

---

[1] Gracieuseté et propreté valent mieux que sale beauté.

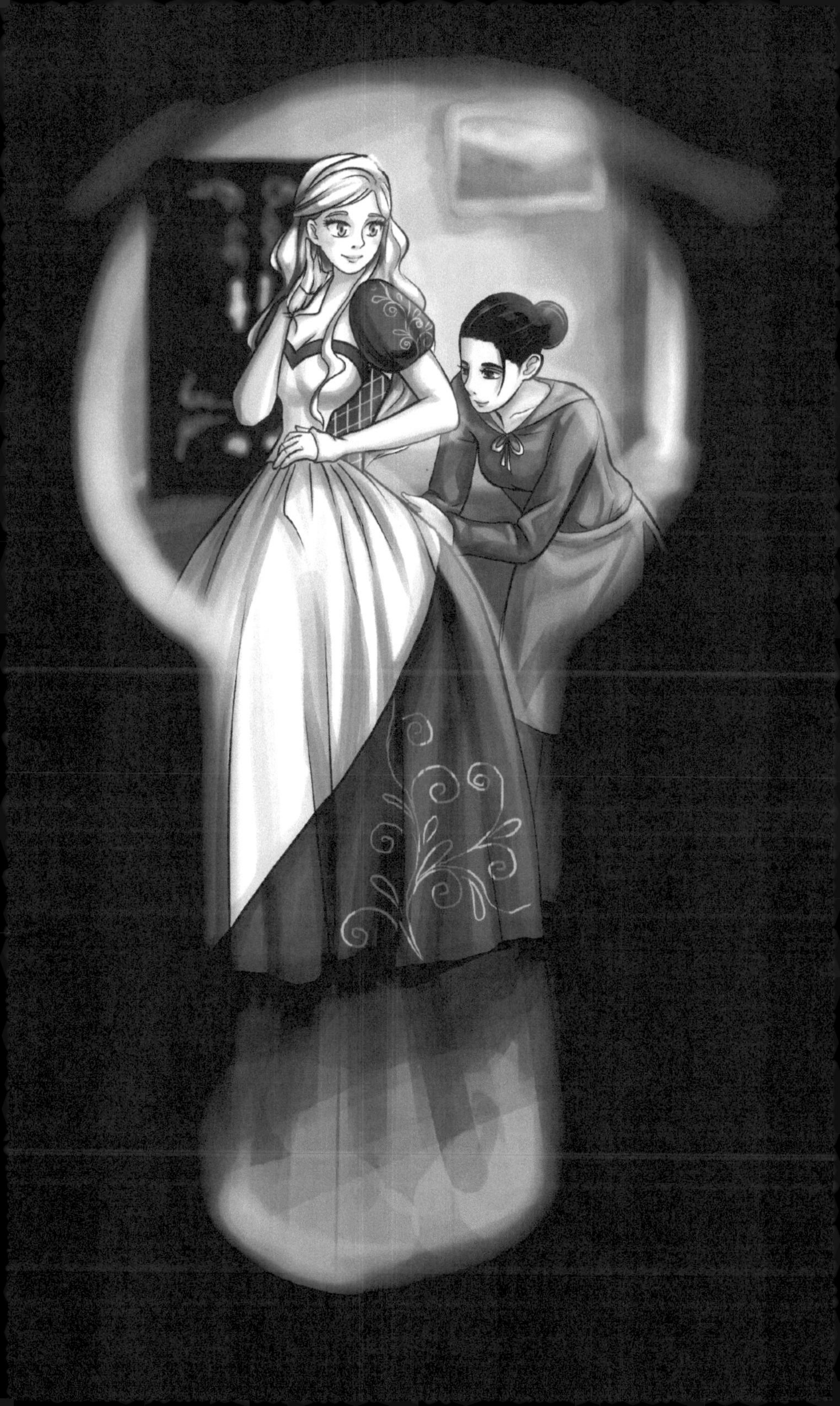

The Mean Joker

THE MEAN JOKER

A joker named Pierre lived in a foothill village. Nobody liked his jokes because they were too mean. When he played a trick on an old woman, it cost her a dozen new gray hairs. When a young boy was the victim, he ended up crying.

Pierre preferred to play tricks on the local strongman Théo. Théo was too kind to avenge.

Once they met near a cliff. The strongman wanted to teach the mean joker a lesson. He stood in a way to obstruct the passage for Pierre.

Pierre realized that there was no way he could make the giant move.

"Can't you see?" he shouted to the strongman. "The rock's going to collapse and crush us both unless you support it right now. I'll fetch a log to prop it."

Of course it was a trick. The rock was firm and steady. But Théo was very credulous, so he leaned against the rock to prevent it from collapsing. In the meanwhile, Pierre escaped. He got away with it again.

When the villagers found out about the trick, their patience snapped. They said, "*To teach a fool is the same as to cure a dead man.*[1]" Yet, they wanted to teach Pierre a lesson to remember.

They got the heaviest log they could find and made Pierre bring it to the cliff as he promised. It took him a dozen of days—long enough for him to realize that a mean trick can be a really heavy burden.

Sometimes the joke is on the joker.

---

[1] A laver la tête d`un âne on perd la lessive.

The Poor Widow, Her Son, and Cabécou the Goat

THE POOR WIDOW, HER SON, AND CABÉCOU THE GOAT

Once upon a time a poor widow and her little son named Charles lived in Poitou Province. The woman had to work hard to earn a crust. Her son tried to help his mother. But, as the saying goes, *poverty writes laws of its own*[1]. When he had grown up, he had to work as a goatherd for a wealthy villager. He had to herd goats, take care of them, and protect them against wicked wolves, who never hesitated to catch a disobedient goatling. The villager usually gave him a cup of milk and a cornpone. He would drink the milk and take the cornpone to the widow. This helped them hold their heads above the water. The master promised to pay the goatherd in the fall provided that not a single animal was missing.

Once a wolf sneaked up on the herd when it was grazing on a green meadow. He caught a young goat and ran away. But Charles was not afraid and ran after him. Whether because the wolf was old and weak or because of the boy's good luck, the goat was alive. She had wounds on her neck and leg, though. Charles began to nurse her. He applied a healing potion to her wounds and gave her freshest grass to eat and purest water to drink. She recovered and grew so loyal to the boy that she always followed him wherever he went. The goatherd even gave her a name, Cabécou, meaning a little goat. When the payment day came, Charles asked his master, "Monsieur, could you give me the goat that I saved from a wolf instead of the money."

---
[1] Necessité fait loi.

"You've been a good worker," said the master. "So I'll be generous to you. You can have both your money and the goat."

Charles brought the goat to his home. The widow was happy to finally have an animal. She began to milk the goat. She produced more milk than they could drink, so they gave some to their neighbors. They still had a lot of milk left. The mother and her son decided to make cheese from it. They fermented the milk, formed small cheeses, sprinkled them with black pepper, and wrapped them in chestnut leaves. Charles brought the cheeses to the market. Everybody praised them, "What kind of cheese is it? It's so soft, savory and delicious!" "It's made of the milk of my dear goat Cabécou," Charles replied. "Please take some. I'll bring more next week." "We'll be happy to buy some," women kept saying.

He sold the cheese for enough money to buy a present for everyone: a new apron for his mother, a bright belt for himself, and a silver neck bell for their breadwinner, the goat.

The mother and her son soon became famous all across Poitou as the best cheese-makers. They became wealthy, bought a big herd of goats and employed several workers to look after them. However, Charles wanted to take care of Cabécou himself because her magic features had made them rich. Charles's young wife used goats' wool to make warm clothes, which Charles's son, deep sea captain Monsieur Jean, has worn with pleasure. By the way, he liked to drink goat's milk as a child. He will always remember what his father said: *"No good comes without work.[2]"*

---

[2] Nul bien sans peine.

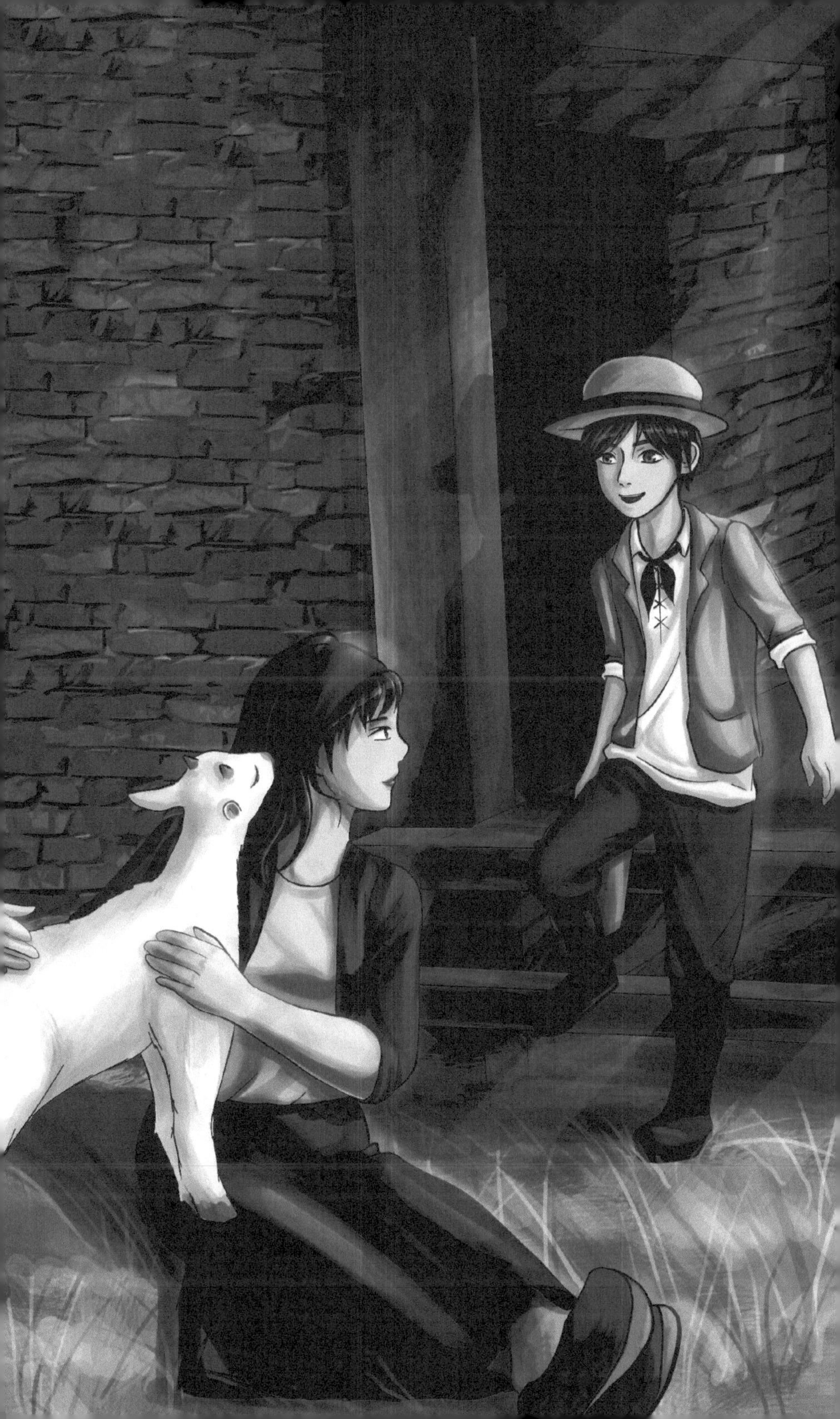

The Pilot from Boulogne

THE PILOT FROM BOULOGNE

I

Once there lived an old retired pilot in Boulogne. He lived with his wife and young son. His pension was too small, so he had to buy a boat and go fishing every day. His son was seven or eight years old. He often asked his father to take him along. But the old sailor was afraid for his only child. The boy was so eager to have a sea trip that he once hid among tackle and sails. When his father had put off, he jumped out and shouted merrily, "Look, Dad. I'm going fishing with you!"

As the boat was approaching the fishing place, the pilot saw a huge foreign ship showing its flag, which meant it wanted to enter the port. When the boat was close enough, the crew asked the fisherman if he was a pilot.

"I used to be one. Even though I'm retired now, I can lead you to the port."

They accepted the old pilot and his son on board. The ship had arrived from the Kingdom of Naz. The country's king had ordered the crew to bring a French boy. They would bring him up in the foreign kingdom and marry to the king's daughter.

When the king's people saw the pilot's son, they liked how healthy and smart he looked. They said, "This is the one we need. We don't have to go any farther."

They gave the old pilot food and drinks and said that he could return to his boat because they did not need him anymore.

The pilot got into the boat and began to call his son. The crew said that his son would stay with them.

The ship departed in full sail, leaving the father in despair, for he lost his only son.

II

The ship arrived in the Naz capital. It saluted the city with twenty-one cannon shots, which greeting was returned. The child was introduced to the king. The king found the little French boy charming. He ordered his people to bring him up as if he was his own son. When the boy turned eighteen, the king married him to his daughter, who was also eighteen years old.

Living in abundance, the pilot's son often though about his parents, "They were not rich when I left them. I'd love to see them and make sure they have everything they need."

He shared the intention with his wife. She thought that it was quite natural and that she should accompany her husband.

The princess and her spouse boarded a ship and soon arrived in Boulogne. The ship saluted the city with twenty-one cannon shots, and the customs guardians checked the ship and informed the authorities that the prince and princess of Naz had come to France for entertainment. The guests went off into a silver boat, which brought them to the shore. They saw all kinds of important people who had come to meet them and offer them the best accommodation in the city.

Surrounded by the glittering retinue, the prince saw an old man wearing a patched sailor blouse. He was leaning against a rickety fence. He recognized the man to be his father, very poor and lonely. The prince burst into tears because he regretted leaving his father. He came up to the old man and asked how he was. The pilot was very surprised to see a silk-clad gentleman ask after the health of a poor man like he.

"Don't you recognize me?" the prince asked.

"I don't, Sire," the old man replied.

"I'm your son, whom a ship from the Kingdom of Naz once took away from you. I'm married to the princess of that country. How's my mother?"

"She's at home. She's very old and sad."

"Cheer up, Father. I'm here to provide you with everything you need."

He returned to the high officials and ordered them to prepare a cabin because he was going to take along his father.

They all returned home and lived happily ever after.

Life before Birth

LIFE BEFORE BIRTH

Nobody remembers this legend nowadays. However, ancient books have brought it down to us. As the saying goes, *What is written with a pen cannot be hacked away with an axe.*[1]

Legend has it that all babies live on clouds before they are born. They can see the whole world from there. It is a splendid view. Just imagine the earliest rays of sunlight, a delicate pink, and the last rays of sunset, a delicious golden. The rainbow shows its colorful curves.

This is the place where all babies wait for their time to come to our world, when they will find themselves in their mothers' lap. Angels take care of them when on clouds.

Angels know exactly when each baby is to be born and never make a mistake. When the right moment comes, an angel flies up to the right boy or girl and touches the baby's lips with his index finger. This leaves a small dimple above the upper lip, and the baby forgets their life on clouds.

The newborn remembers nothing but the angel's beautiful smile. It is like seeds sowed in the heart to yield love, kindness, mercy, and other good qualities.

The angel holds the baby and brings him or her down to earth. Some parents feel so grateful to him for the baby that they name their newborn after him.

Legend has it that the angel who brings the baby to earth guards and watches this person from a cloud for the rest of his or her life. This is how babies are born—an angel hands them over to their parents.

---

[1] Qu'est-ce que la plume qui ne sera pas coupé avec une hache écrit.

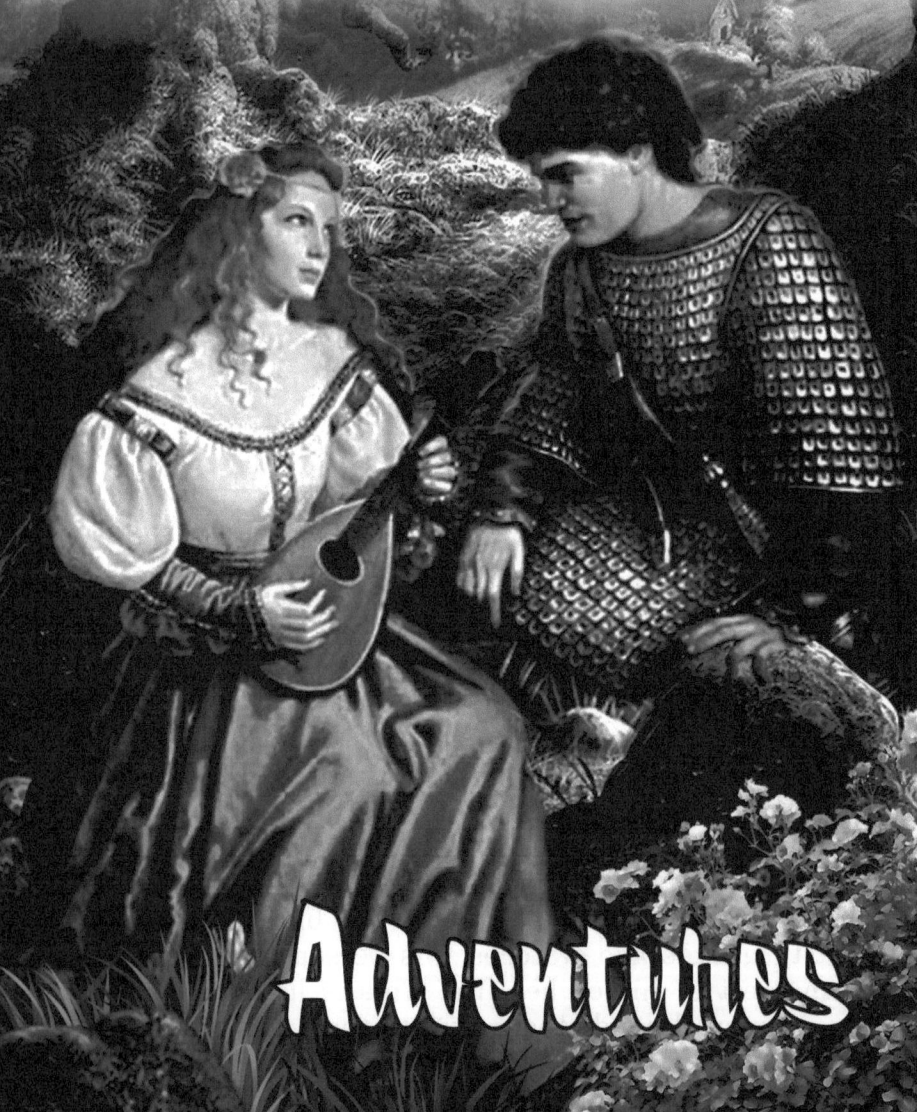

Captain La Ramee's Adventures

CAPTAIN LA RAMÉE'S ADVENTURES

I

Once when Captain La Ramée was traveling around he encountered the Wolf, the Eagle, and the Ant in a thick forest. The three of them were sitting near a killed lamb. They were having an argument because they could not think of a fair way to divide the prey.

At hearing them, the Captain came from behind a tree and said, "Come on, friends! Can't you solve the simple problem?" "No, we can't, old man," the three animals replied. "You're so experienced. Can you help us divide our prey?"

The Captain grew thoughtful. Then he unsheathed his sword and said while waving it, "You Wolf get the four legs. You Eagle get the bones. You Ant can have the head."

"Now this is fair! What kind of a reward would you like?"

"I'd just love to be friends with you!" the Captain said laughingly.

"Alright," said the Wolf, the Eagle, and the Ant happily. "All kinds of things can happen. Bear it in your mind that you can always turn into a wolf, or an eagle, or an ant—whichever you like. You only have to shout, "Wolf, be my brother!" or, "Eagle, be my brother!" or, "Ant, be my brother!"

Captain La Ramée said thank you.

II

He entered a town on his way. All people were sad there. They were discussing something in whisper and crying.

Surprised, the Captain asked a very old woman, "Why is everyone crying? Has a misfortune befallen you?"

The old woman explained, "It has. It's been a year since a wicked monster stole our merry Jeanette, the King's daughter. Many a brave man have tried to save her. It cost them their lives because the Princess is locked in an unapproachable castle on a steep rock. The monster itself guards the castle. Nobody has been able to kill the monster because its life is hidden in a magic egg."

"What kind of an egg is it?" asked La Ramée.

"It's charmed, Captain. It holds the monster's power. Neither a sword, nor an arrow, nor water, nor fire can damage it. But it will die if you break the egg. Many heroes have tried to get it, but nobody came back."

"I think I should try," said the Captain.

III

He shouted, "Eagle, I want to be your brother!" In a moment, he had wings. He flew up high to the rock and crossed the tall castle walls.

He saw awful fire-breathing dogs at the entrance.

"Wolf, be my brother!" shouted La Ramée and turned into a wolf at once.

The wolf did away with the wicked guards and ran to the tower door. It was locked, so La Ramée had to call his third friend for help, "Ant, be my brother!"

Hardly had he finished when he became a black ant small enough to enter through the keyhole. He ran into the locked room through wall cracks.

In the middle of it there was a big table with a chest of gold on it.

It was then that Captain turned back into a human being. He unsheathed his sword and cut the lock off the gold chest. There was an egg, harder than stone and blacker than iron.

La Ramée broke the egg and heard the monster scream as it died.

The brave captain had to walk all around the castle to find the poor princess in the last tower. She was crying and shaking with fear, waiting for the awful monster to come. When La Ramée entered the room, she could not believe her eyes.

"Who are you?" Jeanette asked in a breathless voice.

"I'm Captain La Ramée. I came here to set you free. The monster is dead. You may go!"

This is why the city of Bourget has such a beautiful coat of arms.

How Sheep Crossed the River

HOW SHEEP CROSSED THE RIVER

The King had a taleteller. He often told him amusing stories. The King could not even go to sleep without a good tale.

Once he went to bed and called for the Taleteller. The Taleteller began his story.

Once upon a time the King sent for his Taleteller, who was already going to sleep. He was too tired to tell tales.

"Your Majesty," he said, "it's too late for tales. Can I tell you one some other time?"

The King grew angry. He wouldn't go to bed without a new tale! The Taleteller had to obey.

"Once upon a time, Your Majesty, there was a man who had a hundred gold coins. He decided to buy sheep for the money. He bought two hundred sheep and drove them to his village. When he was approaching the river, he saw that if had flooded the whole meadow. Unfortunately, there was no bridge. How could the sheep cross it? Suddenly, he saw a boat. Only it was so small that it could only carry one sheep."

The Taleteller broke off. He was too sleepy to continue.

"Go on!" the King grumbled. "What did he do to the rest of his sheep?"

"Your Majesty!" the Taleteller replied. "You kindly know the river to be wide, the boat small, and the herd as large as two hundred sheep. It will take them long to get to the other bank. Let's sleep while they are doing it. I'll tell you the rest of the tale when they have crossed the river."

Vivienne and the Sun

VIVIENNE AND THE SUN

Once upon a time there lived a girl in Provence. Her name was Vivienne. She went to a village school.

One day the teacher asked the class where the sun rises, in the east or in the west.

The best pupil said confidently, "I know that the sun rises in the east."

This is what the rest of the class said. The teacher praised everyone.

Only Vivienne kept silent. So the teacher said, "Now you, Vivienne. Where does the sun rise, in the east or in the west?"

Vivienne answered, "I disagree with the other pupils because *the Sun does not rise. It is the Earth that travels around the Sun.*"

The rest of the class didn't like her answer because it was different than theirs. They began to grumble at her.

But the teacher said, "In fact, Vivienne is right. Bear it in your minds, children, *that strength lies not in force but in truth*[1]."

---

[1] Force n'est pas droit.

Jean the Fool

JEAN THE FOOL

A village boy was so stupid that people called him Jean the Fool.

Once his mother sent him to the market to buy a swine. Jean the Fool chose one. He paid for it and showed the way to the swine, "Now you're mine, Piggy. Go home! This way."

He had a nice long walk around the place and left for home, too. His mother asked him, "Where's the swine?"

Jean the Fool told her what had happened.

"You foolish little thing! You should have put a rope on its leg. You hold it tight and beat the swine when it gets off the road."

"Alright. I won't fail next time."

Jean's mother asked Jean to buy a pot on the following day. Jean the Fool bought one, put a rope on its handle, and pulled it home. The pot cracked on a stone. He only brought the handle on the rope.

"Where's the pot?" Jean's mother said in a surprised voice.

"I did what you had told me, but the pot wouldn't come along."

"You foolish little thing! You should have put it on your back and watched your steps!"

"Alright. I won't fail next time."

On the following day Jean's mother asked him to buy a large piece of butter.

Jean the Fool carried it on his back in the middle of the treet, watching his steps carefully. The sun was hot. The butter melted all across his back. When Jean came home, his mother asked him, "Where's the butter?"

Jean the Fool showed her his back.

"You foolish little thing! You should have put the butter into a bag lest the sun should melt it. You dip it into water every once in a while so it doesn't get soft.

This should be the end because I couldn't tell you about all foolish things that Jean the Fool did even if we had as much time as it takes to walk to Paris.

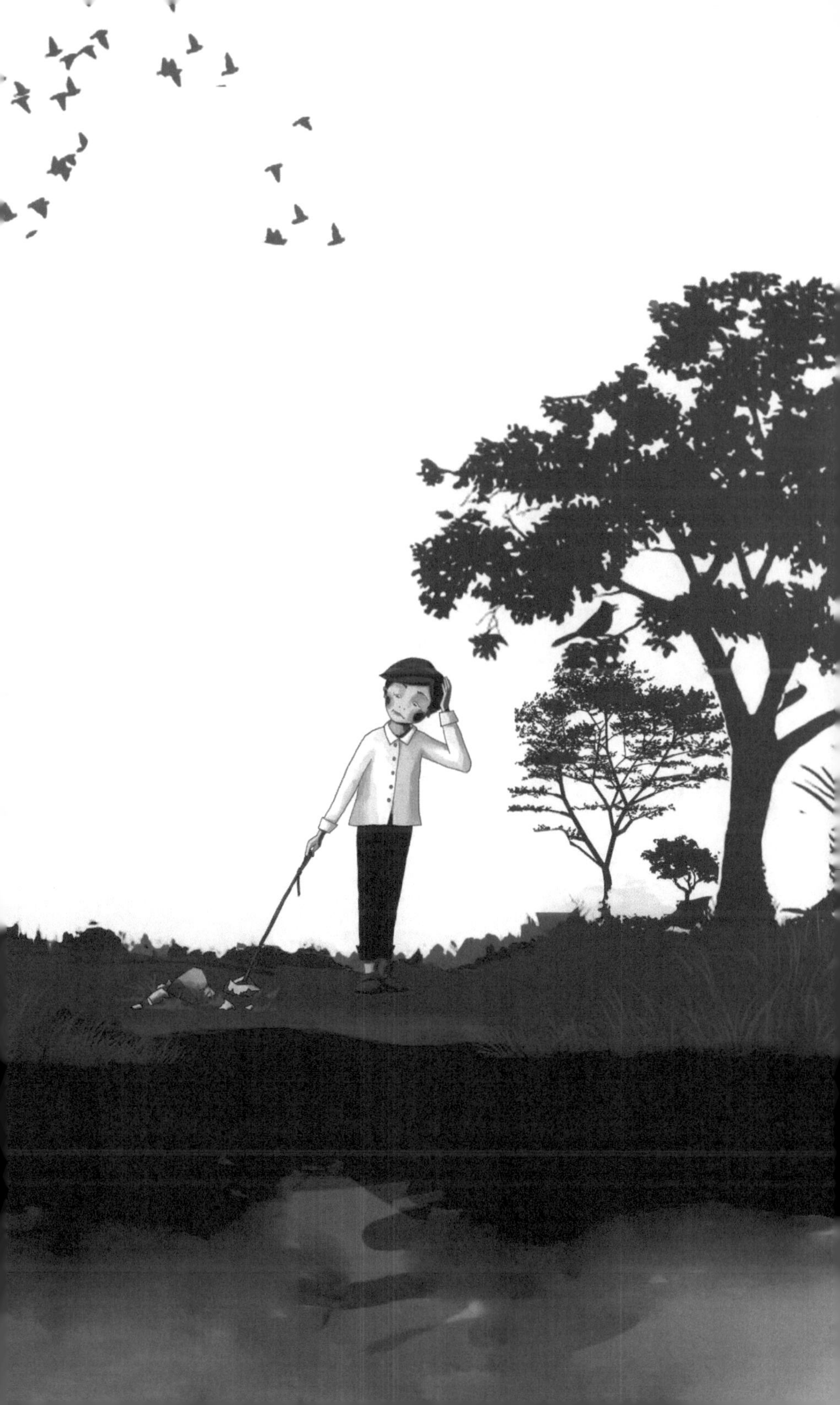

The BEAUTIFUL PRINCESS, The BRAVE KITTEN, and The DRAGON

THE BEAUTIFUL PRINCESS, THE BRAVE KITTEN, AND THE DRAGON

The beautiful Princess lived in an unapproachable castle on the sea shore. Every day her waiting ladies accompanied here to the garden, where the red Kitten lived in a hollow old apple tree. The Princess would stop to play with him and offer his something tasty—cream or a piece of fresh fish.

It was a wonderful summer morning. The air smelled of lavender and roses, and a fresh wind was playing tag with snow-white clouds. The Kitten woke up, stretched, and went to the garden. A strange green log was lying on a flowerbed. He sneaked up to it cautiously and touched the log with his paw. Nothing happened. Then he gave it a scratch. The Kitten was very brave.

"Ouch!" said the log, opening a sly blue eye, "Why are you scratching me?"

"You smell strange!" the Kitten hissed with an angry meow. "This is my garden! I don't need talking logs here!"

"I'm not a log. I'm the Dragon!"

When he saw the giant monster with his mouth full of teeth, the Kitten got very scared. But it was his garden and his favorite flowerbed, so he fluffed up his tail and showed his teeth.

"Wow!" the Dragon said in a surprised voice. "Such a brave little thing!"

"What are you doing in my garden?" snorted the Kitten.

"I'm waiting for the Princes," the Dragon replied.

"Why do you need the Princess?"

"We dragons have to have a princess," the monster sighed. "If you don't have any, you are not a true dragon. This is a proper one. Lace dress and a crown on her pretty golden locks."

"So what are you going to do to her?" the Kitten asked. He thought that the Princess was his and would not let the Dragon have her.

"Nothing," the Dragon shrugged his shoulders. "I'll just bring her to my cave and boast to other dragons."

"Your cave?" the Kitten was surprised. "Princesses don't live in caves. They need a soft bed, sweet porridge for breakfast, and waiting ladies to teach them how to wave their fan and turn around when wearing a dress with a train."

"Nonsense!" the Dragon said strictly. "I have a decent cave, no quilts and disgusting porridge! I'll steal the Princess and make her sleep in a basket and eat raw meat."

The Kitten said with a sigh, "You won't enjoy her company for a long time then."

"Why?"

"She'll get sick and die."

"So what?" snorted the Dragon. "I'll show her to other dragons before she dies."

The Kitten grew sad. He did not want the Princess to die such a disgraceful death. He though, "*Nothing is impossible for a valiant heart!*[1]"

"Why don't you steal me?"

"You're not a princess!"

"I'm much better," the Kitten said with a sly purr.

"Why?"

"I like to sleep in a basket, I'm not afraid of caves, and I love raw meat."

---
[1] À cœur vaillant rien d'impossible.

"This is not enough," the Dragon said thoughtfully.

"I'm soft. I can purr. I like to play. And I can catch mice!"

"It's good but not enough!" the Dragon shook his head and touched the Kitten cautiously. "You're really very fluffy!"

"What is more important," the Kitten came very close to the Dragon, "stealing Princesses is out of fashion! But I'll grow to be a big cat. No dragon has a cat like this."

The monster thought for a while and said, "You're right! I don't care about the Princess! Get onto my back and be careful not to fall down!"

The Kitten glanced around his garden and the old apple three that had been his home, sighed, and jumped onto the Dragon's back. Adventure was waiting for him. Maybe he would even come back to the garden.

The Princess was very sad to know that her waiting ladies could not find the Kitten. She ordered them to leave a treat near the apple tree every day. She found it untasted day after day. But once it was gone.

Who knows, maybe a brave little thing lives in the hollow again...

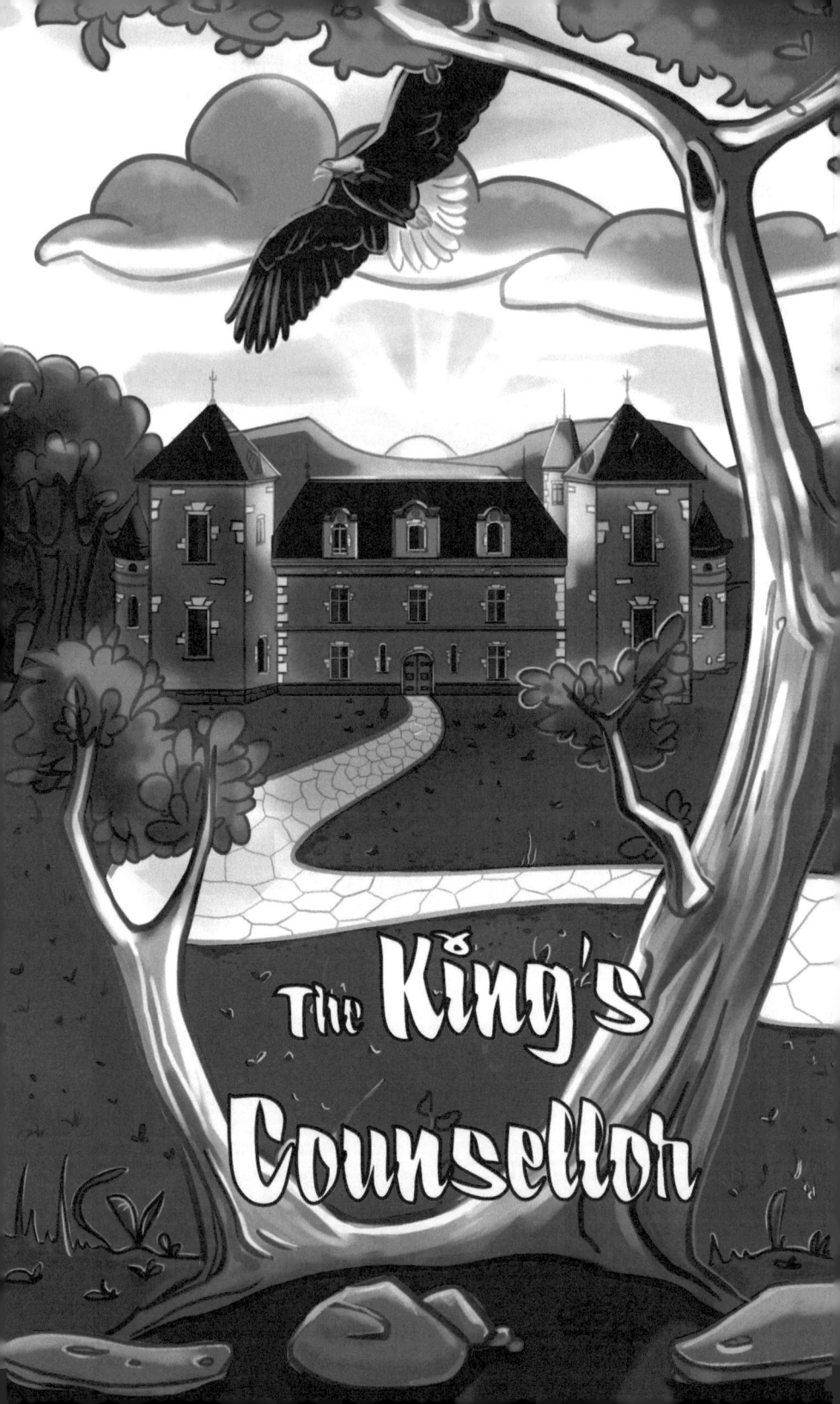

The King's Counsellor

THE KING'S COUNSELLOR

I

Two brothers lived in a small village. The elder brother was smart and brave. His name was Pierre. Pierre always had wonderful ideas. He invented an air balloon to travel with. He also designed a three-wheel bicycle.

The younger brother, Arnie, did not like to talk. He was modest. Being a very simple chap, he did simple work. He made baskets, repaired clothes and shoes, grazed cows, and collected honey. He would often do something for free for his poor neighbors. A cup of milk and a piece of bread was enough for him.

So they lived. Pierre invented, made drawings, and read a lot. Arnie worked hard and helped him build his inventions. Once, the King learned about the elder brother's talent. He sent a messenger to invite the smart man to be his counsellor.

II

Pierre was happy and proud. Arnie made him wonderful clothes and shiny leather boots to match the occasion. They set off together because they had never been apart for a moment since they were born.

They walked for a long time across fields and woods until they reached a large meadow with a leaning old hut on its margin. A crooked old man came out to welcome the brothers and offer them rest and food. They were very tired, so they were happy to agree. It was a hot day, and they could hardly discern the walls of the palace on the horizon.

"Give us a lot of water to wash our faces and lay the table," Pierre ordered.

"I've got only a cup of water left," the old man shrugged his shoulders. "The heat has dried away the near brook, so I have nothing to water my flowers and crops with. I began to dig out a well, but I'm too weak... You'll have as much clean water as you want by evening if you kindly help me."

"You silly old man," Pierre said with a laughter. "I am going to be the King's counsellor. How can you offer me to dig the ground? I could give you a valuable advance to make your everyday work easier for you. But are you worth it? I'd rather have a rest so that I can look really good when I meet the King."

III

While the smart brother was sleeping on fragrant hay, Anrie took a spade and helped the old man dig the ground. It was a hard work, but they could see cold clear water on the bottom of the well when the sun began to set. It was enough both for the lonely master to water his vegetable garden and for the brothers to wash their faces. As the two of them, clean and well-rested, were going to say goodbye to the old man, he said, "Don't you hurry. You have already found what you are looking for."

He threw aside his shabby cloak and old straw had, and the brothers were astonished to see the King. He was wearing a crown of gold on his well-groomed golden locks.

"But this is the King!" Pierre said with a gasp and blushed heavily.

The King was a generous man. He did not punish the proud-hearted brother and let him go in peace. The younger brother, Arnie, received an ample award for his kindness. The elder one, Pierre, will always remember what the King said. He said, "*Advice is good, but help is better,*[1]" and "*Do good without resting and telling anyone, and your time will come soon.*[2]"

---
[1] Conseil est bon, mais aide est encore mieux.
[2] Fais bien sans cesse et sans demeure, en peu de temps se passe l'heure.

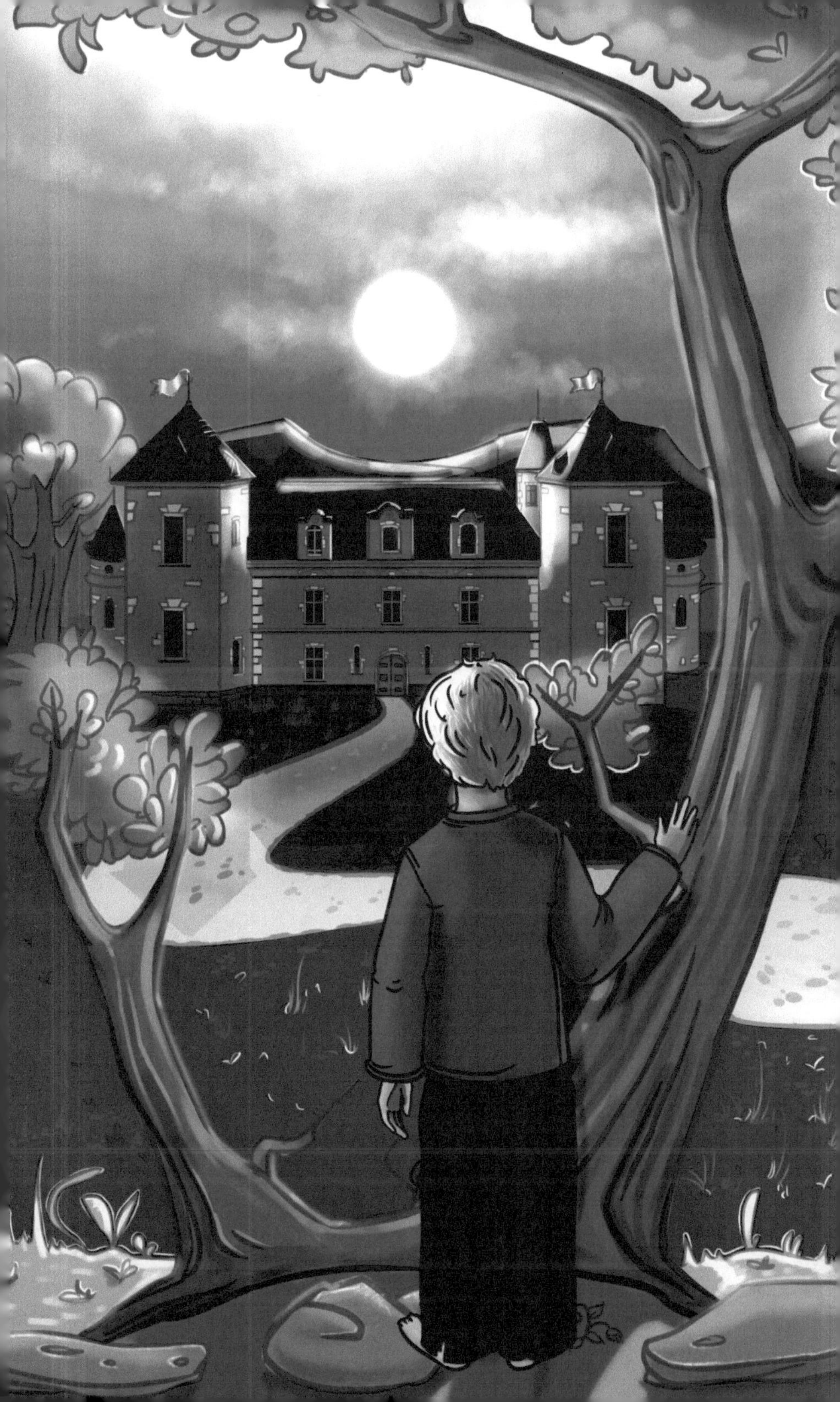

How the Caterpillar Turned into a Butterfly

HOW THE CATERPILLAR TURNED INTO A BUTTERFLY

Once upon a time, there lived a green Caterpillar. She did nothing but eat green leaves and grow even greener. But once she started to feel bored.

"Everybody has fun—some fly from flower to flower, others leap from leaf to leaf or dig new tunnels. I can only crawl and chew."

At hearing her say so, other caterpillars said, "You're wrong! Everyone has a destination. We should be true to ourselves."

This made the Caterpillar feel rejected and lonely. She hid in a dark corner and thought, "I'll make a nice cocoon for myself and stay here forever. I can't stand my boring life anymore."

So she made a cocoon, crawled into it, and cried herself to sleep.

When she woke up on a chilly morning, she knew that her sadness and grudge were gone. The Caterpillar wanted to come back to her family and friends. So she got out of the cocoon.

Nobody recognized her, and she did not know why.

"Could they have forgotten me while I was asleep?" the Caterpillar thought in surprise.

Suddenly she startled with fear. A creature of unheard-of beauty was looking at her from inside a silvery dewdrop. She had large intricately shaped opalescent wings.

The curious Caterpillar came closer to the dewdrop. She could not believe her eyes when she realized who it was. "It's me! My reflection is looking at me! A miracle happened to me when I was asleep! Look how wonderfully beautiful I've become!"

The Caterpillar flew with joy, fluttering her new pretty wings. She danced with colorful flowers and was happy to be as beautiful as they were.

"Butterfly is my new name!" the Caterpillar said to her friends.

Life is full of miracles. You should bear it in your mind that *to want means to be able*[1].

---

[1] Vouloir, c'est pouvoir.

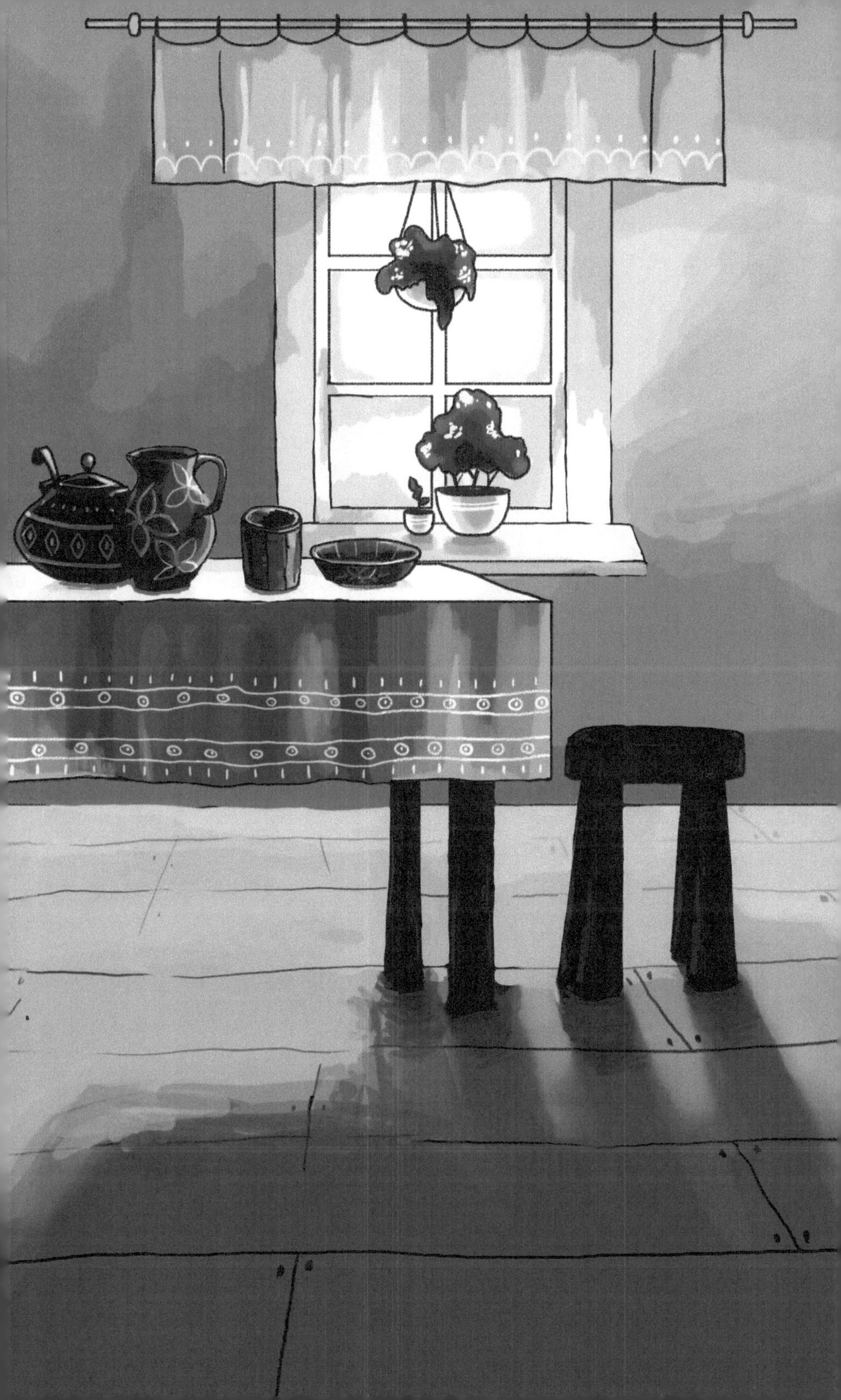

The Bear and the Fox

THE BEAR AND THE FOX

Once as the Bear was strolling in the woods, the Partridge happened to fly right into his open mouth. The Bear pressed his jaws together and walked on. He was happy because he had a sure meal.

The Fox happened to be passing by. Seeing the Bear with the Partridge in his mouth, she decided to take her away. She invented a way of deceiving the Bear soon.

"Dear Neighbor," she said to him, "Could you tell me from where the wind blows?"

The foolish Bear should have said, "From the west." That would make his teeth even tighter. But he said, "South." His mouth opened, releasing the Partridge. The Fox jumped and caught her.

"It blows from the south, alright," she said laughingly and ran away, leaving the Bear open-mouthed and hungry.

The Fox and the Tit

THE FOX AND THE TIT

Once upon a time, the Fox was having a walk in the woods. She was starving, so she decided to look for some sparrows. The Fox forgot to watch her steps and fell into a deep pit.

"There's no way I can survive here. I'll die of hunger soon," the Fox thought with terror. "I have to think of a way to get out."

The Fox began to shriek and beg for help. The little Tit heard her. She glanced into the pit and saw the Fox crying.

"Hey there, why are you crying?"

"I'm crying because I've fallen into the pit and can't get out on my own. Will you help me?"

"Look at me! I'm so small! How can I help you? And what if you get out just to eat me?"

"You can bring some tree branches. I'll pile them up and climb them. I won't hurt you if you help me out."

It took the little Tit three days to fetch enough branches. When the Fox finally climbed the top of the pile, she remembered how hungry she was and leaped at her. Tiny as she was, the Tit was agile. She dodged the attack and grabbed a small branch from the bottom. The pile shook and fell apart. The Fox was back in the pit.

She begged tearfully for help, but not a single animal would listen to her. They left the Fox to die in the pit because she was mean.

The Hedgehog and the Chestnut Shell

THE HEDGEHOG AND THE CHESTNUT SHELL

A very long time ago, when trees were so tall that they touched the sky, a chestnut tree grew in a forest. Nobody paid any attention to it. It was just another tree.

In fall a strange spiky nut prickled the Squirrel on the paw. "Ouch!" the poor Squirrel screamed.

The nut fell onto the ground. Its shell cracked, and a smooth shiny chestnut rolled out of it. The news traveled fast. Many animals came to see the strange nuts because it is always interesting to see and try what one has never come across.

The little Hedgehog had very short legs; so he was the last to come. He found nothing but prickly shells under the tree. "If only I had a coat like this!" the Hedgehog said with a sigh. "Nobody in the world would hurt me!"

Hedgehogs didn't have their prickles at that time, so the Fox often caught them.

The Fox was there in no time. He did not like nuts at all but knew he could find something for dinner.

Everybody noticed the Fox and ran away. But the Hedgehog was too sad to see him approach.

"Well, well," the Fox said with a clatter of his teeth. "What a soft little thing!"

"Help!" the Hedgehog screamed.

"No need to scream." The Fox grinned.

The Hedgehog wanted to back away but stepped onto a chestnut shell. It turned round in the air, capping the Hedgehog.

The Fox opened his mouth and took a bite. The whole forest could hear him scream, "Ouch! It hurts so badly! It's unfair! My tongue hurts me!"

Glancing from under the shell, the Hedgehog said, "Go away! You're not welcome!"

He passed his tiny paw around the shell. It was only prickly on the outside. Its inside was as smooth as silk.

"You'll be my coat," the Hedgehog decided.

The shell agreed silently. The Hedgehog made better company than a heap of fallen leaves after all.

"*Need makes the old wife trot*[1]," the Fox grumbled every time he saw the Hedgehog. He did not attack him again, though.

This is why all hedgehogs have prickles. If some of them are larger than a chestnut shell, it just means they have a healthy appetite.

---

[1] Le besoin fait la vieille trotter.

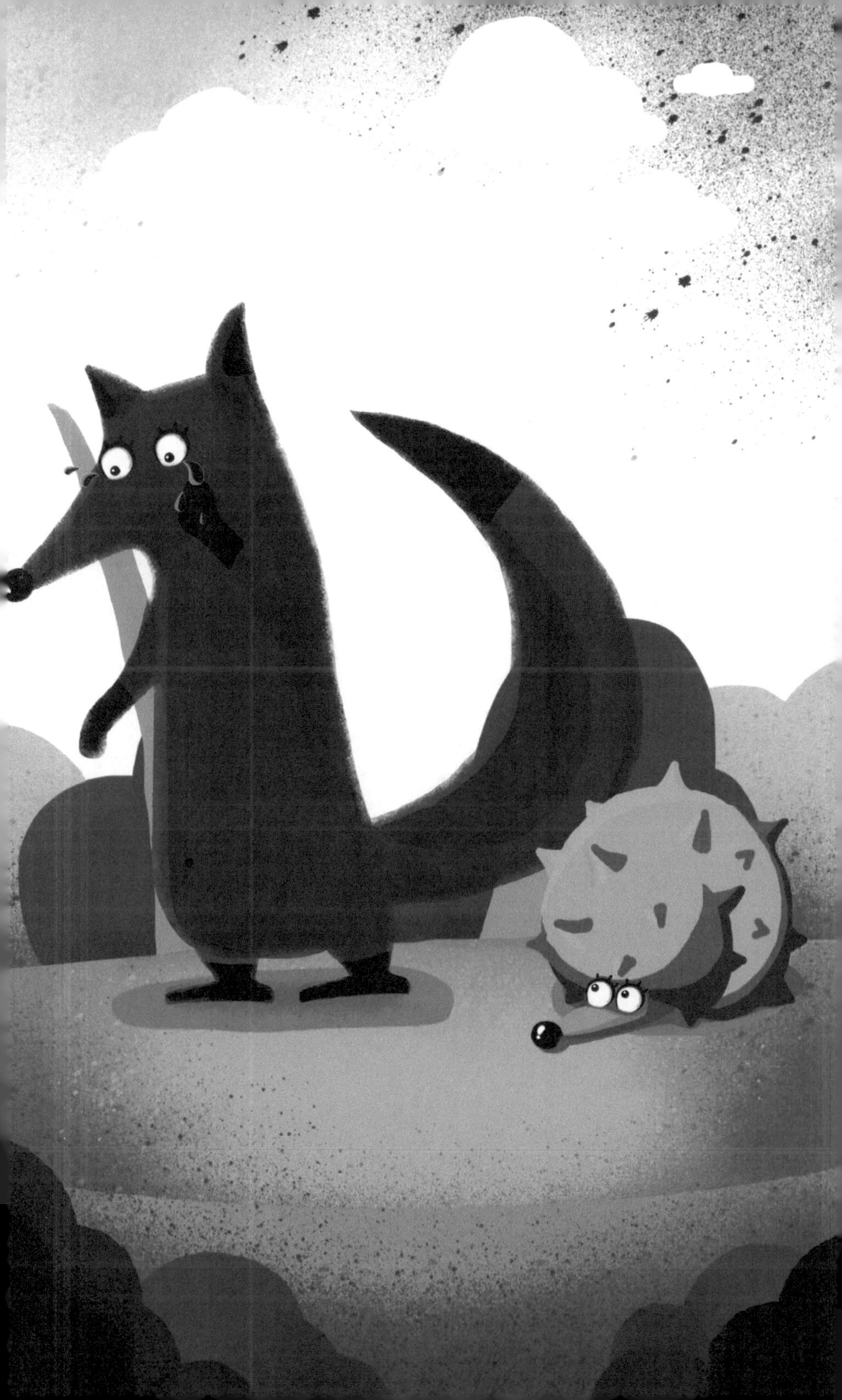

Biron

BIRON

I

Once upon a time there lived a man called Biron. He spent days walking around the city, wearing a top hat. Everybody believed his top hat to be made of pure silver.

One day Biron invited two stranger dandies to an inn. The innkeeper often gave Biron meals on credit and even lent him money.

After a square dinner, Biron took off his top hat and began to turn it round and round in his hand. While doing so, he kept saying, "Everything has been paid for in full!" "How come?" the dandies asked amusedly. "My top hat has already paid for the treat. Ask the innkeeper if you don't believe me. Am I telling the truth?" Biron asked the innkeeper. "Of course you are," said the innkeeper without batting an eyelid.

The two dandies exchanged winks—they'd love to buy the funny thing—and began to beg Biron for the top hat.

"I like it a lot," Biron said, pretending to be upset. "But I'll sell it to you for as few as a hundred gold coins."

II

The dandies were happy to get the top hat for a hundred gold coins. They wanted to test its magic and called at another inn.

After a most substantial meal, they began to turn the top hat round, saying, "Everything has been paid for in full."

"Don't you talk nonsense. Where's the money?" said the innkeeper.

"The top hat has paid for everything!" one of the friends said proudly.

When the innkeeper grabbed a stick to hit them, they could not buy pay.

They rushed out of the inn, cursing Biron, "What a fraud! We should teach him a lesson."

The friends headed for Biron's house.

III

Biron was on the alert. He knew that he had fooled the two dandies and that they would not leave him in peace. So he cooked some soup and put the pot with the bubbling soup in it over the embers. Just in time! The dandies rushed in to see Biron. He was sitting by the fireplace with no fire in it, stirring bubbling soup in a pot. They were amused to see the soup boiling without any fire.

They forgot about their indignation. They wanted to know everything about the pot.

Biron explained it to be magic. He said that one could use it to cook without any fire. Amused, the friends bought the pot after a little bargaining.

When at their place, they put some raw meat into the pot and put it over the fireplace without making fire. They waited for the meat to be cooked for a long time. At last, they broke the pot to pieces and shouted, "Death to Biron!"

IV

They ran to his home, pinned his hands to his sides, put him into a bag and dragged it to the river bank to drown him for his nasty tricks. It took them some time to recover their breath.

"Let's have a drink in the nearest inn," said one of them.

"I don't mind."

They ran to the inn, leaving the bag on the bank. Of course, Biron heard them speak, so he began to shout, "I don't want to marry the King's daughter!"

A mule skinner was passing by. Hearing Biron shout, he ran up to the bag and asked him "Hey there, is it true that you don't want to marry the King's daughter?"

"Of course I don't. I'm not the right man for her."

"So get out of the bag and let me marry her."

"I will. Only open the bag."

The mule skinner opened the beg. Biron got out of it, helped the mule skinner in, and tied it tightly. He drove the mules away.

Having returned to the bank, the friends heard, "I agree to marry the King's daughter!"

"No way!" they said laughingly, "You'll get what you deserve!"

They grabbed the bag and threw it into the water. "Off with Biron!" they said.

V

Relieved, they went home. All of a sudden, they saw Biron walking along the road, driving a herd of fat mules. They ran up to him and asked, "Have you really got out of the river?"

"Why, can't you see?" he smiled. "Thanks for putting me there, though. There's a fair under the water. That's where I bought these mules for a fairly low price."

"Do you think there are any goods left?"

"Sure. But you'd better hurry!"

"Right," the friends said. They did not hesitate to plunge into the river.

Nobody has seen them since then.

***

The latest version of the book
in a hard copy can be found
at the following locations:
www.amazon.com/dp/1792730764
www.amazon.com/dp/170376997X
www.amazon.com/dp/1651023417

Jean the Thumbling, the Wolf, and the Robbers

JEAN THE THUMBLING, THE WOLF, AND THE ROBBERS

I

A poor woman had three sons. They were very pretty. But the youngest one was as small as a thumb. So his name was Jean the Thumbling.

Once Jean went to the woods to pick some berries. A hungry Wolf decided to eat some. Some wolves fed on berries back then. He did not even notice swallowing Jean the Thumbling as he devoured a bush.

II

So Jean found himself in the Wolf's throat. In the meanwhile, the Wolf looked for more food. He sneaked up to a pound. All of a sudden, Jean the Thumbling shouted, "Hey there! Shepherd! Sheep! Take care! There's a wolf!"

At hearing this, the shepherd began to chase the Wolf with dogs. The Wolf got some sticks and bites. He hardly reached the forest.

Every time he tried to eat a sheep, Jean the Thumbling prevented him from doing so.

Tired of starvation and beating, the Wolf asked the Fox for advice.

"I'm the most miserable animal ever. I've got something in my throat that screams each time I want to eat a sheep. Shepherds attack me, so I can't eat. I am going to die of starvation."

The Fox was very cunning. She lowered her head and closed her eyes, pretending to be thoughtful. Then she opened her eyes and said in a smart-sounding voice, "I think I've heard about such an ailment. Some of us foxes once had it, and some of us foxes cured it. Don't be afraid. I'll help you out. Can you see these two trees growing so close to each other? Push your neck between them as tight as you can so that you can get the screaming thing out."

The Wolf pushed his neck between the trunks until it felt really tight. He began choking but could not get out. He thrashed so heavily that he tore his head off. The Fox was happy to have played such a nasty trick on the Wolf. She disappeared in the woods.

III

Jean the Thumbling appeared from the Wolf's throat. He climbed a very tall tree to see if he could find the way back home. All of a sudden, three robbers came and began to part their pillage. It consisted of old coins.

"This is yours. This is his. This is yours."

"No. This is mine!" Jean the Thumbling shouted from above.

The robber thought that his friend was complaining and said, "Enough for you, you fool."

As they went on, Jean the Thumbling kept shouting, "This is mine!"

The robbers got scared and ran away, leaving the coins under the tree.

Seeing the coins, Jean the Thumbling thought, "I wish I could take them home." But he did not know where his home was. Suddenly his mother turned up. She had been searching for Jean since the day that his brothers left him in the woods.

She hugged her dear son and kissed him, crying with joy. "My chicken! I've found my chicken!"

Jean the Thumbling hugged her back, saying, "Mommy! Mommy! We'll always be together!"

Made in United States
Troutdale, OR
09/22/2023